Teardown

CLEA YOUNG

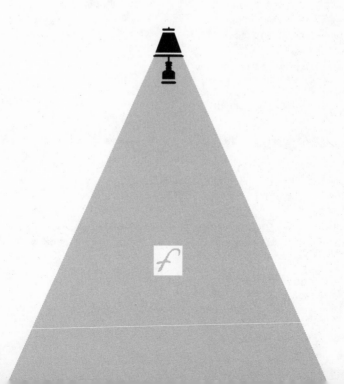

Freehand Books gratefully acknowledges the support of the Canada Council for the Arts for its publishing program. ❡ Freehand Books acknowledges the financial support for its publishing program provided by the Government of Canada through the Canada Book Fund.

Canada Council Conseil des Arts   Alberta
for the Arts   du Canada   Government

Freehand Books
515 – 815 1st Street SW Calgary, Alberta T2P 1N3
www.freehand-books.com

Book orders: LitDistCo
100 Armstrong Avenue Georgetown, Ontario L7G 5S4
Telephone: 1-800-591-6250 Fax: 1-800-591-6251
orders@litdistco.ca
www.litdistco.ca

Library and Archives Canada Cataloguing in Publication

Young, Clea, 1977–, author
Teardown / Clea Young.

Short stories.
Issued in print and electronic formats.
ISBN 978-1-988298-01-6 (paperback).
ISBN 978-1-988298-04-7 (html).
ISBN 978-1-988298-05-4 (pdf)

I. Title.

PS8597.O582T43   2016 c813'.6   C2016-903513-1   C2016-903514-X

Edited by Barbara Scott
Book design by Natalie Olsen, Kisscut Design
Author photo by Théodora Armstrong
Printed on FSC® recycled paper and bound in Canada by Friesens

TEAR DOWN

For my parents, with love

Teardown
1

Split
15

Dock Day
29

Chaperone
39

Juvenile
59

Lamb
73

*Congratulations
& Regrets*
97

New World
121

Desperado
139

Ursa Minor
163

Firestorm
187

*What Are You
Good At,
What Do You
Like to Do?*
209

Teardown

Teardown

WE WERE THE COUPLE having a domestic on Saturday afternoon in IKEA. We might as well have been on stage, we were that well-lit.

"We came for a crib," I said, "not a chandelier."

"This is a pendant lamp," Mari said.

Another couple, young and fresh, edged past us. They exchanged a we-will-never-be-that-couple look.

A month ago Mari and I had moved out of our one-bedroom apartment and into a two-bedroom house of approximately the same size. We were still renting. In other words, the house wasn't ours, so why bother with new fixtures and roman blinds? It was going to be torn down — maybe as soon as next summer — and we'd be left with a bunch of crap that might or might not work wherever we landed next.

Mari was running her hands over her enormous belly. I didn't want to make her cry, to be the guy who makes his pregnant wife cry, but come on.

"You're being impulsive," I said. "We don't need this. We need other things, but not this."

Mari lifted the box from the shelf and opened it to make sure the rattan shade was intact. She removed the protective cardboard and tossed it aside. Then she yanked the shade from the box and swung it by its cord.

"Whoa, whoa," a store employee said. "Can I help you?"

"No, thank you," Mari said. She looked down her nose at the woman who wasn't just short but tiny in every way; she might have been playing dress-up in the boxy store uniform. Mari, on the other hand, was statuesque, what people call big-boned. Her posture, her curves, demanded attention. Pregnancy had only placed her further outside the realm of ordinary human beings. Wherever we went people stopped to stare. But the employee was neither intimidated nor amazed.

"What are you doing with that lamp?" she said a little too curtly for someone whose designation is customer service.

Mari sighed. "Getting a sense of how it will look above our table."

"There are showrooms upstairs, where you can get a *sense*," said the employee. "These are fragile. You don't just whip them around."

Mari looked at me. "Am I whipping this around?"

"Well . . ." I said.

The employee tried to grab the cord from Mari's hands but Mari was too quick, too tall. The shade swung back and into a display of energy-efficient light bulbs.

I crouched and began gathering up the packages at Mari's feet. "She's not going to wreck it," I said.

"Oh?" the employee said. "Seems like a bit of a loose cannon to me."

"Do you talk to all customers like this, or just pregnant ones?" Mari said.

The employee rolled her eyes.

"What was that for?" Mari said.

"You're playing the pregnancy card?"

Mari forced a laugh. "Did you really just say that?"

4

The smug couple now stood a few feet away, gawking. A mother and her university-age daughter also slowed to observe.

"We're not getting that piece of junk anyway," I said.

"Yes, we are," Mari said. She dropped the shade into our cart, then picked up another two boxes, each containing the same product, hucked them in after. She went recklessly for a fourth but the employee stopped her, moved between Mari and the bin.

"Now you're just being crazy." The employee looked at me and said, "Put the brakes on her, would you?"

"Oh my god!" Mari said.

"Everyone knows customer service can be brutal," I said, "but you've crossed a line."

"*I've* crossed a line? Yesterday someone crapped in one of the display showers."

"Okay, Juliana," I said, crouching to get a look at her nametag, "that's disgusting. This is hardly the same thing."

"You're all capable of it," Juliana said.

"So are you, if you want to get right down to it." The conversation was getting ridiculous. I wanted Mari to jump in again. I reached for her, for where I last knew her to be standing, slightly behind and to my left, but my arm swiped at air. She was gone. Her purse was still in the cart. I picked it up and turned the soft leather over in my hands.

"It's pretty obvious," Juliana said. "She's gone to complain."

I wasn't so sure. She would want me for backup, nodding at her shoulder as she recounted Juliana's offences to Customer Service.

I had Mari paged. Her name sounded out over the heads of hundreds of shoppers and not one person looked up. If a child were missing this place would be on lockdown. And in fact a child *was* missing, *my* child who still needed a crib but whom I couldn't actually picture in said crib. I'd never even held a baby before. I'd seen other men jiggling small bundles, sometimes in one hand, their free hands digging bus fare from pockets or stabbing at platefuls of eggs in busy breakfast restaurants. I would need both hands, possibly even a third to hold my baby, this much I knew. Just thinking about it made me shaky. I told the woman at Customer Service I'd wait for Mari in the cafeteria.

In line, I remained on my toes, alert, looking out over the hungry hordes, expecting Mari to appear at any second, panting slightly, wearing the sweat moustache she sprouted so easily these past months. I ordered two hot dogs and a sugary drink flavoured with synthetic pear, and found a table squished between families, children bucking in high chairs.

"Let mommy eat her food," said a woman through clenched teeth. "Mommy needs energy to deal with you."

I imagined our unborn child sitting quietly with the picture book I would bring along for just this sort of situation. I imagined giving him bites of Swedish meatballs when Mari wasn't looking. We would be allies, me and the little guy, whose sex, though still undetermined, I was certain of. I had difficulty imagining a squalling baby in our lives, but for some reason I could easily picture a toddling boy. I saw us creeping from the house weekend mornings, leaving Mari to sleep. We'd go wherever he wanted and we wouldn't need a stroller. He'd just wrap his arms around my neck and we'd head out, sandwiches and a thermos of hot chocolate in my knapsack, maybe a ball to kick around.

I sloshed the last mouthful of carbonated drink around my mouth, revived. "Excuse me," I said to the families. I was hemmed in on all sides. A woman tugged a high chair aside without looking at me. "Thanks," I said, and rose onto my toes;

the floor around the high chair was bombed with tidbits of spinach crepe. "Hi, buddy," I said as I inched past the baby. He smiled manically, his goopy hands reaching for the crotch of my jeans. A man I guessed was the father jabbed at his phone. Mari and I would not be like these parents; we'd be super-engaged.

I relocated to a bench near the women's washroom where I watched the women go in, heard toilets flush and the hand-dryer blasting, then watched the same women exit, clean hands tucked inside shirtsleeves. It made sense that Mari would be in there; we often joked our baby had moves, imagined him breakdancing on her bladder. But unless something was truly wrong, she'd be out by now. Eventually I enlisted help. The woman was blonde with thin lips, dressed in a drapey grey sweater, dark jeans, and tall suede boots. Officious, like she could deliver the news.

"Pregnant," I said. "Hard to miss."

"And yet she's missing," said the woman slowly.

"Well, yes. I mean, no. We've been separated. Not *separated*. We've just lost one another."

The woman swung through the washroom door and seconds later came back out.

"Not there."

"You hardly looked."

"The stalls are full. They're in use. No one's holed up in there, okay?"

I had Mari paged again. This time Juliana appeared and sat down on the bench next to me.

"She hasn't turned up?"

I said nothing.

"I feel vaguely responsible," she went on.

"Vaguely?"

"Look, I *may* have overreacted. Anyway, I want to help."

I wondered if she'd been hired *because* she was so small, if size was a consideration in affirmative action. Her feet swung above the ground and her pants had been rolled several times into bulky cuffs. I couldn't actually tell how old she was, still a teenager or in her mid-thirties.

"Let's hear it, "I said. "What's your plan?"

"We comb the place. If we're thorough we'll find something."

"I don't want to find *something*. I want to find Mari."

"That's what I mean."

"Don't you have a job to do?"

"No one will notice I'm gone."

"Because you're—"

"Because I'm what?"

"Nothing."

We split up. I took the showrooms while Juliana flipped through the racks of hanging carpets and other places she'd known people to hide. Was Mari hiding? I wasn't convinced. I wandered through the jigsaw of sofas, surveying the women reclining upon them, testing cushions for that crucial marriage of durability and comfort. I imagined finding Mari asleep on a loveseat, curled in the position of our baby inside her. I imagined rubbing her back till she woke, face marked with fabric, fabric marked with drool. The lamp was fifty dollars. It wouldn't break us. I touched the arm of each loveseat I passed but Mari didn't appear. I stumbled on to an expanse of dining tables, beige and off-white linens set with indecipherably different versions of tableware. I sat and placed my elbows on a table, head in my hands. Mari loved tablecloths and heavy cutlery. She lit candles every night, even if we were just eating takeout. Would she still do that after the baby was born?

"That painting, for example," she'd said when we were sitting down for dinner last night. She pointed to the canvas leaning against the wall. It had been there since we moved in. Mari had started the nail but said the picture was too heavy. "Doesn't it bother you just propped there?" She flicked the lighter but the spark didn't come. She flicked again and again until finally I grabbed it, shook it before her face. "It's almost empty. You have to shake the fluid into the valve."

"I like matches," Mari said, picking up her fork and jabbing it in the direction of the painting, wanting to get the conversation back on track.

I tried to explain that the same things weren't as urgent for me. I urgently wanted to rig up our hammock on the porch to catch the last freakishly warm blasts of autumn. I had urgently wanted to kill the ants swarming the back patio, which I eventually did with kettles of boiling water and strategically placed pucks of Raid.

"Anyway, this isn't our home, Mar," I said.

"I guess we should keep our dishes in boxes, too?"

I wanted to say something equally snarky: pregnancy glow was a myth; her nightly cocktail of prenatal vitamins didn't cancel out her morning intake of caffeine; I hated that painting anyway. Instead, I pounded the nail into the wall and lifted the damn thing into place. We ate the rest of our meal in silence. Between us, flames like pricked rabbit ears.

I had liked our centrally located apartment with heat and hot water included. I didn't like that I now had to think about the duration of my showers, that our neighbours remarked on our arguably overgrown lawn. Mari liked having two bedrooms, a yard, and a washer and dryer. Apparently these were things you needed when you had a baby. I pointed out that babies all over the world lived in one-room huts and slept with their siblings and parents in one great big bed. Mari said most would prefer otherwise. How did she know?

"She's not here," Juliana said, nudging my elbows from the table and straightening the place setting before me.

I picked up a wineglass and spun the stem between my fingers. The crowd of shoppers had thinned. It was getting late, but without any windows it was hard to say just how late.

"I know," I said. "Thanks for looking."

"Maybe she went home," Juliana offered.

I pulled Mari's purse from my lap. "Wallet, and keys."

"That *is* troubling."

I shoved back my chair and started the way I'd come, through the maze of three-walled showrooms, so many options, so many tidy possibilities for people's lives. Mari wanted one of these arrangements. She wanted everything just so before the baby was born. How many times did I have to tell her the baby wouldn't know the difference?

"I even checked the ball room," Juliana said, tripping at my heels. "Once a guy refused to come out until his wife agreed to let him choose the hardware for their kitchen cabinets."

"Hmm," I said.

"The *ball* room," she repeated. "Over the *hardware*."

"I heard you the first time."

"I haven't checked the warehouse," Juliana said. "You could do a few laps through there."

There was no reason for Mari to be at the warehouse, another compound across the parking lot, but what choice did I have? There were more shopping carts than cars outside now. They were strewn across stalls, set adrift as customers made their getaways. Two men in company-issued blue and yellow coveralls were using leaf blowers to create piles around the perimeter of the lot. Another couple of employees followed, gathering the leaves and punching them down into giant paper bags. Maybe Mari had decided to leave me. In the rice paper glow of IKEA she couldn't *not* see my inadequacies, the terrible father I was about to become. Or maybe something really had happened to her. While I'd been arguing with Juliana a couple who couldn't have children of their own had abducted her, held a knife to her side, and locked her in a basement with flickering lights to await the birth of our child. Either way my wife was missing. I had to call the police, her parents. I made fists and pushed them against my eyes until bright colours began to spin kaleidoscopically behind my lids. I thought about the jars Mari had sterilized this morning in preparation for making applesauce, something the baby could eat when the time came. I thought about how she spent her evenings now, studying the stages of labour and grimly laundering and folding sleepers, bibs, and booties that barely fit over my thumbs. I hadn't shown enough interest in these preparations. At our last session with the midwife, instead of asking how I could support Mari in labour, I'd wondered aloud if I might get a turn on the nitrous oxide. Would there be an extra bed in Mari's hospital room for me to rest? A quick look of disbelief passed between Mari and the midwife. I should have let it go, and I cringed now recalling the fight I picked once we were outside the uterus-coloured walls of the midwife's office: I was an equal player in this production, why shouldn't I also get support during the delivery? I turned away from the warehouse and began to run toward our truck. I would drive the surrounding blocks while I made the appropriate calls. I would check gas station washrooms and patchy roadside bushes. But first I would demand that these ex-con-looking leaf collectors empty their bags. I unzipped Mari's purse looking for the keys and spilled its contents at my feet. Then I tripped and did a face plant just inches from our rear bumper. Above me, someone sighed. The lightness of it filled in my chest like a balloon. I lifted my face from the pavement, spitting gravel from my tongue.

"Took you long enough." The voice was coming from the bed of the truck. I strained toward it, grabbed the bumper, and hauled myself up. I saw a pair of argyle legs. Mari's tights. She was lying on her back, knees raised. I dropped the tailgate with a bang. Mari looked around the stupendous mound of her belly. "Lip's bleeding," she said.

I stuck out my tongue and tasted blood. I couldn't think what to say. I felt as if I'd been ganged up on, Mari and the baby, two against one.

"My back was killing me," Mari said. "Come here."

I crawled in beside her and rested my head on her shoulder. She sniffed my hair. "Our child is never eating hot dogs."

"I know," I said. "And only organic."

"You found her." Juliana, in civilian clothes, peered over the side of the truck. "Security's checking the surveillance videos," she said, "which is clearly unnecessary. You had him pretty scared."

Scolding Mari was unwise. "I was worried," I said, "it's true. But everything's okay now. Is your shift over?"

"Yeah." Juliana jerked her head at a minivan pulling into the lot. As it rolled toward us I saw a man in the driver's seat and some little hands waving in the back. I couldn't make out if the man was her husband or her father, the child her sibling or her own. "See you," she said.

"Doubtful," Mari said.

"Mar," I said. "Come on." Then to Juliana I said, "Have a good night."

We were quiet for a few minutes after she left. I knew Mari was deciding whether or not to be mad. I didn't care what she decided. I pulled a strand of her hair from my mouth and nuzzled into her neck. I'd always hated the metallic smell of her unscented, hypoallergenic face lotion, but at that moment I savoured it, I drank it in.

"I'm sick of people telling us how much our lives are about to change," Mari said finally. "As if we don't know."

"We don't, Mar, not really."

"It's the *way* they say it."

"What if I'm a terrible dad? What if I don't know how to comfort the baby, or you?"

"I have to get this baby out of my body, that's what I'm worried about right now."

"Women are giving birth all over the world, every second of every day."

"And airplanes are taking off and landing. It doesn't make me any less scared to fly."

"What if I told you your body's designed to do this."

"Still not reassured."

Mari shivered. The sky was the last shade of grey before black and stars. Vertiginous.

"It'll all be over soon," she said, which was both true and untrue. I sucked my lip and thought of the tiny red being inside Mari, ear to the wall, taking stock of our ineptitudes, weighing the future in his perfect mind.

Split

Split

ALANNAH AND CASE have a one-year-old and insist that Tova and Jed be *their* guests so the baby will have its toys and comforts on hand should he grow fussy. Fine, sure, Tova agrees, though the baby is a messy one and, consequently, the house is too. Tova knows they will end up eating from plates in their laps. Sure, fine. Though her Saturday-night-self prefers a candle-lit table and a good red in a globular wineglass. There is also Case and Alannah's dog, Sadie, a standard poodle. She is dread-locked and smart. And though it hasn't always been this way, much of an evening with Alannah and Case is spent discussing genius — the baby's and Sadie's — and sending Sadie outside so she'll ring the doorbell and wipe her paws upon re-entering. Tova can never get it straight: talk at one, walk at two? Alannah and Case are always saying things like, "You should get yourselves one." Meaning a baby.

TOVA LIES BACK in the tub, a wet face cloth covering her breasts. It's something she remembers her mother doing and so it's become one of those inexplicable habits carried on. Tova remembers, too — it wasn't so long ago — when she and Jed were inexperienced lovers in one another's arms. How even amid their ungainly groping, Tova managed to hide from Jed her split left nipple; whenever her shirt came off, her hand became a shell to cup her breast. Tova peels the waterlogged cloth from her chest and regards her anomaly. She's unsure if split is the correct word. Perhaps inverted. Maybe mutant. Her nipple has since become a joke she and Jed share; when it's soft, it looks like a mouth with no teeth. Yes, they laugh about it now. Privately though, Tova wonders if it will cause problems if, or when, she has a child and wants to breastfeed. What if the nipple doesn't work? What if the breast becomes full but the baby cannot drink from it and it grows painful and huge and must be punctured so that the trapped milk (might it sour inside her?) can flow?

Tova drains the water from the tub. She smears cream on her legs and rubs the excess into her elbows. Even though her mother offered no counsel on the matter, Tova is sure Jed is her first and last husband. The same way she's sure that when she overturns a rock at a certain beach she'll find a crab snapping its pincers. It was strange, though, for her mother to have kept silent. Unnerving after so many years of advice, wanted or not, to abandon Tova to her own shaky will at the point of such a crucial decision. She's sure she made the right decision marrying Jed. Feels empowered having come to it on her own. Maybe this was what her mother wanted for her. Tova calls Jed her tangible man. In the kitchen, she hears the spinner as he whirs lettuce for a salad they will take to dinner. He sings "Piece of My Heart" in his scratchiest, most rock-and-roll voice, which is gentle, barely audible above the watery flush of the spinner.

TOVA LEANS AGAINST the kitchen door jamb wrapped in a towel. With his back to her, Jed slides a disc of flour-dusted pastry onto a pie plate, then slops in diced apples. Cinnamon. Jed is a culinary whiz. And so relaxed as he moves from cupboard to stove to fridge. He can carry on a conversation while he cooks, adds ingredients that aren't called for in a recipe but end up improving the dish. Tova is spastic around vegetables and knives and pots of boiling water. Everything burning or wilting or dissolving. Jed has tried to teach her some tricks: mince, don't press, garlic (to avoid bruising the juices); massage kale with olive oil and lemon juice (to give the leaves a softer texture). But Tova is too impatient to learn. Whenever she tries, she and Jed jolt about from counters and cutting boards and into each other. Inevitably, Tova grows angry with Jed's precision and ends up where she is now, standing in the doorway.

"What are you making?" she asks.

"Hey babe." Jed doesn't turn or look up.

"Alannah said to just bring salad."

"I know. It's for the little guy." Jed shapes the excess pastry into strips and arranges them in letters on top of the pie.

"Tiger?" Tova asks, leaning over his shoulder to read.

"That's what Case calls him." Jed squeezes in an exclamation point so it's Tiger!

"I don't think he can eat solids yet."

"You're missing the point, babe. It's for Case and Alannah. To show them that we like, I mean we *care* about their child."

"Well, they'd have to be idiots to think we don't." Tova turns toward the bedroom. "The way you goo-goo-gah-gah all over it."

JED WOULD LIKE to have children and Tova would like him to have them. His arms are made to rock babies, to swing them dangerously high and catch them just in time. Only Tova hasn't yet fallen under that maternal spell she's heard women speak of so rapturously. And so she must wait either until she falls or is pushed headlong into its deep, embryonic darkness.

Until then, she will use Alannah's baby as a gauge. Tonight Alannah will offer her the baby and Tova will receive it with tentative arms, attempt to calm her racing heart as she jigs the squirming bundle. She doubts anything will have changed. When Tova held the baby as a newborn her mouth dried up and she began to sweat. The baby wailed bloody murder. How could a floppy-necked rag-doll channel such a sound?

"**THOSE WERE GOOD** apples," Tova says. "I wish you hadn't used them in a pie."

She's dressed casually, but not without care, in slim-fitting jeans and a new sweater, pulled her hair into a high ponytail so the baby won't unexpectedly, or expectedly, depending on who you are, tangle his fists in it. "Not all apples are good for eating. Those ones were tart and crisp. The kind I like."

"I'll buy more tomorrow," Jed says.

"Some apples are fibrous and soft," she continues, "like they've already started to decompose. I'm just saying, those are the kind to cook with."

"Leave it alone," Jed says. Tova realizes she's been picking at a pimple on her chin and drawn blood. The spot was barely visible when she discovered it in the bathroom mirror a few minutes ago and squeezed and poked in an attempt to extract some impurity from the dark pore. She does this, blotches up her face before she has to be somewhere. It isn't entirely unconscious, but still she can't help herself. Self-mutilation, her mother called it. Only a mother would be so extreme.

"**CASE GOT CALLED IN**," Alannah says when she opens the door, baby on her hip. "He's sorry, but he couldn't say no." The baby wriggles in her arms.

"No worries," Jed says.

"That's too bad," Tova says.

Alannah's house smells. Like meat, garlic, diapers, dog.

"Hey, Tiger," Jed says and widens his eyes. Alannah sets the baby on the floor and he weaves dangerously, unsteadily through her legs.

"Have you seen him do this?" she asks. "He's not even one yet."

Jed crouches and the baby teeters toward him.

"I don't think so," Tova says. Walk at one talk at two, walk at one talk at two, she chants to herself.

"No," says Jed. "We definitely have not."

THE FIRST TIME Alannah met Jed, she turned to Tova and whispered, "You've mined a gem from the Arctic-fucking-Circle; looks like he'll be a demon in the sack." Tova had never been one for searching out those kinds of men. She'd never thought of men like that—as good or bad lovers. Jed was luck. Jed was deliberating in the produce section at her neighbourhood grocer. When she tells the story of how they met over a bin of Brazilian navel oranges, Tova emphasizes navel, and thinks of a kumquat protruding from her belly button. Alannah was right, at first there was no need for costumes or gadgets. The track of Jed's tongue like snail-glue over her body was enough.

ALANNAH WEARS LEGGINGS, an oversized T-shirt, and the earrings Case made for her birthday, hoops that grow progressively smaller toward the centre, a map's topological representation of a mountain. From the earrings Tova guesses Alannah must have decided, before Case was called away, that it was her night to have a few drinks. Though with Jed here neither Alannah nor Tova will have to lift a finger for the baby. Jed will be down on his hands and knees for hours, for however long the baby can keep its eyes open, playing with blocks and balls. Or he will sit the baby on his knee, hold onto its fragile upper body and give it gentle, crazy-horse rides. The baby will go mental with excitement and they will all laugh and admire its simple baby glee. And then they will admire Jed's way, Jed's natural way with the little guy, as he gives it a bottle and rocks it in his arms, his perfect cradle musculature.

"I just thought it felt like one of those nights," Alannah says, pushing a wooden spoon around a pot of ground beef, carrots, and onions. Potatoes boil on another burner; the starchy water steams the black windows. "Shepherd's pie. Comfort food, you know? It's still blustery out there, isn't it?"

"Power's out in a bunch of places," Jed says.

Comfort food? Blustery?

"Everything's changed so fast. At the park today, leaves were coming down, honestly these yellow leaves were . . . I could cover my entire face with one, which he loved." Alannah nods at the baby, who sits in the middle of the kitchen looking up at his mother, a string of drool connecting his chin to the grimy linoleum. "What kind of tree would that be anyway?"

"Couldn't say," Jed offers.

"Want a beer?" Alannah asks. "There's wine, too."

"Wine for me," Tova says.

Jed says, "I'll drive."

"I didn't say I was going to drink the bottle." Every time she has a drink Jed assumes, or Tova assumes Jed assumes, that's the end of her. Blotto for the night. Practically passed out and puking. That's how it makes her feel when he pulls out his "I'll drive" line so early in the evening.

"Red or white?" Alannah asks.

"Whatever's open," Tova says. "Just whatever."

TOVA HAS KNOWN Alannah since before the baby, since before Case, when, during their first year of university, they worked at an Italian deli in a neighbourhood shopping plaza. It seems impossible that the Alannah before Tova now, grating cheese onto a shepherd's pie, is the same girl with whom she deftly crushed boxes by a dumpster. Seagulls bitching overhead; always a cigarette hanging between Alannah's lips; always a dirty monologue on whatever party she'd been at the night before, the blundering guys who'd tried to win her attention. Her arms rose reflexively with each stomp of her Doc Martens. "Don't dance me into a dark corner, don't get me another beer. Ask me a question or two." Tova studied Alannah as though she were a course subject. They worked in glorious tandem behind that cramped deli counter, serving the line of aproned workers from the grocery store wanting their lunch, and fast. But here, in Alannah's home, they're out of step. Or Alannah is. Tova studies her with the same intent, not to emulate Alannah this time, but to catalogue her decline: she's restrained, hunched. Where is her old, rough grace?

"**SOMETIMES I WANT** dirty. Sometimes I want to be goddamn spanked," Alannah said one night when she and Tova went for drinks, before the baby, when Alannah and Case had been together a year. Tova hadn't heard from Alannah in almost two months so she dropped everything to see her. They sat tucked in a horseshoe booth at a high table. Tova loved the way Alannah swore, effortlessly, without giving a profane word any more or less weight than a pronoun. She loved when Alannah reached across the table and grabbed her wrist, for emphasis.

"He's not taking risks, what does that say this early in a relationship?"

"Jed bites sometimes," Tova offered.

"Bites? Where?"

"Once he bit my ass."

"God, if only." Alannah sighed and relaxed into the cushiony velvet. That night Alannah wore pink fishnet stockings. When she took Tova's hand and raked it up her leg to demonstrate just how Italian, how taut the threads, Tova felt it was her own leg she was caressing.

TOVA EYES THE baby where he stands on shaky legs, holding on to the lip of the coffee table. Jed sits behind him, spotting as though from the edge of a trampoline. He's just changed the baby and now it wobbles about wearing only a diaper. Tova has heard at this stage they're practically all organs. The bulge starting beneath the baby's chin and puffing down into his diaper is crammed with lungs, stomach, kidneys, liver. Tova imagines an adult-sized heart beneath the baby's roundness, the person he will become dormant in that pumping muscle. She looks for the "cuteness" she thinks she should see, scans for the pitter-patter her own heart should feel when he releases an impromptu smile. She feels slightly reassured that her own mother never cared much for other people's children. It wasn't until she had Tova, she said, that she understood all the fuss.

Alannah drops cushions around the coffee table and spreads a spattered rag for the shepherd's pie. The baby, swaying at the table's edge, reaches for the hot pan. Even though there's no way his stubby arm can reach it, Jed takes the baby's little fist in his own and pulls it gently back. The baby grunts and swivels his head to look at Jed. Jed beams.

"Oh, candles," Alannah says and disappears into the kitchen. When she returns with two tea lights Tova says, "How romantic." Jed glances at her sideways.

"Dig in," Alannah says. She settles on a cushion, lays the baby across her lap, and lifts her shirt. Tova is still surprised by the brown smear Alannah's nipple has become, no longer the tight star she remembers from sunbathing. The baby's mouth tugs and tugs.

"Hungry guy," Jed says, and Alannah smiles in response. A smile of contentment or complacency; either way, Tova hates it. Alannah's bobbed hair swings forward as she looks down at the baby sucking the life out of her. Sitting like this, long legs folded beneath her, sinewy arms curled around the baby, Alannah still has the body of a ballerina, but now it's the body of an injured ballerina.

"This is good," Tova says. "Delicious."

TOVA'S MOTHER NEVER dropped her on her head. She sent Tova to her room only once. When she visits, she kisses Tova's cheek and pauses a moment to nuzzle her hair, breathe in the familiar smell as she did when Tova was a girl. But her mother has never been one to address the female body's more intimate functions. In her youth, Tova had friends whose mothers took them for lunch or bought them gifts when they started menstruating. And even though Tova scoffed at such rituals, she remembers feeling slightly cheated by her own mother's indifference to her coming of age. When Tova finally got her period at fifteen, a box of maxi-pads magically appeared in her room. Initially, she was grateful to her mother for sparing them both the awkward words, but now, looking at the baby sprawled across Alannah's lap, Tova thinks her body's vocabulary is coming up short.

ALANNAH TAKES TOVA'S hand and pulls her onto the porch, the way she used to guide Tova in and out of nightclubs or nudge her through a day at work. In the bed below, sunflowers metronome on decomposing stalks. No petals, just mushy heads. Sadie has followed them out. She snaps her jaws at each blast of cold air.

"God, I need a smoke," Alannah says, then qualifies, "only when I drink." Alannah has had one glass of wine.

"Sure," Tova says. She watches Alannah struggle with the lighter behind her cupped hands.

"Want one? They're kind of stale."

"No, thanks," Tova says, for no reason other than to deny Alannah's offer.

"So how are you and Jed?" Alannah asks. "You guys seem good."

"We are." Tova can't bring herself to confide in Alannah. To tell her about yesterday when she got her period after a week of thinking it might not come. About how she sat on the toilet and laughed aloud. She withholds the part about Jed's hands on her, how she can predict their patchwork movement up her thighs toward her breasts even before he's walked through the door.

"You guys are good, that's obvious enough," Tova says and reaches for Alannah's cigarette. She doesn't want the inhale; she wants the place where Alannah's lips have touched to touch her own. She sees Alannah as though from a great distance, then her perspective shifts and she sees Alannah as a strange creature at a rare closeness.

"A baby doesn't make it better, though." The words whip from Alannah's mouth and are gone. "I'm sure you can see that for yourself. And the power you have, so suddenly, it's

26

frightening. Sometimes when I'm holding him I think, I could drop him or roll him down the stairs. I could just open a window and toss him out." Tova stares at Alannah's hoops, circles inside circles, each its own orbit. She thinks of the last time they went out, just the two of them, tucked in the horse-shoe booth. Alannah might have been pregnant that night. But unaware of the rosy bean in her womb, she spoke loudly and drank too much. Finger-combed her blonde hair and re-leased the loose strands onto the floor without discretion. That night, too, Alannah declared she was so highly sexed, all she had to do was cross her legs and she would orgasm. And she did, right there in front of Tova, the tables around them full, a line of waiting customers huddled inside the restaurant entrance.

Alannah takes the cigarette back from Tova, draws deeply, and shakes her head. "Obviously I'd never do it," she says. "But just the fact that I could." Tova can tell Alannah's needed to say this for a while. She knows, too, that she should comfort her friend, open her arms when Alannah asks, "Do other moth-ers feel like this?"

Instead, Tova says, "I wouldn't know." She only knows who Alannah was before: a girl who didn't wash her makeup off before falling asleep, who didn't need sleep, who climbed a cinder block wall to skinny dip in an apartment complex's pri-vate pool. A girl who told another girl, hesitant to take off her clothes, worried about flashlights and angry residents, to stop being so scared and enjoy it for what it was: water on every inch of her skin.

"You should call me when you feel like that," Tova says, but Alannah must hear the flatline in her voice. Alannah shouldn't call her. Ever.

JED APPEARS IN the kitchen window with the baby. He rubs a hole in the steamy glass, holds up the baby's fist, and makes him wave. The baby looks out blankly and with lovely ambivalence. And then they are gone. The baby and Jed disappear. Lights snap off inside the house and the houses all around. There is only the wind as it touches down in backyards and retreats. There is only the wind trying to force the trees into each other. Tova looks up to where wisps of cloud cruise steadily and without obstruction. Sadie rings the doorbell and the baby lets out a small shriek inside.

"Luke," Alannah says and rushes toward the door. She flings the cherry of her smoke off the porch and for an instant it is the sun, or some fiery planet going down.

Dock Day

Dock Day

THE CHILDREN GALLOP in and out of the muddy shallows while their parents sip icy drinks on the dock. Every so often the adults plunge their prehistoric bodies into the lake and call out to the children — What sort of trouble are you getting into over there? "There" being the stand of saplings whose roots grow into the water, where the children are arguing who among them will be king and queen.

"I'm the oldest," says the boy who knows about castles and kingdoms.

"I'm the only girl," says she with the braids and runny nose.

The king picks elderberries and places them on a bark plate. Death berries, he calls them. Whoever has committed treason must eat them.

"Treason?" says the queen.

"Lied," explains the king.

"I'm not playing," says one boy, though he doesn't make a move to leave.

The only other boy, the youngest of the four, sucks in his cheeks, holds the flesh between his teeth.

"**THIS MOLE.** See, here?" says Anne. She covers all but her nipple and points to a mark beneath her breast.

"Whoa, I'm being flashed," says Tom, the man not her husband.

"God, it's just a breast," says Anne.

"But it's not attached to my wife, understand? There are rules about this kind of thing, there are—"

"Yeah, your wife's are way nicer," says Anne. "Now look, it's a little red. It could be cancerous but my husband here doesn't seem to care."

"Of course I care, but go to a doctor instead of polling our friends," says Dallas, Anne's husband. "This is the fourth time you've whipped it out."

"You make it sound like a mutant appendage." Anne snaps her bikini back into place.

"How can you say mine are nicer?" says Rebecca. She runs her hands over her chest, rendered plank-like in her sportive one-piece. "The kids ruined them, turned them into 'saggy little prunes,' as I seem to recall someone saying."

Tom scans the shallows. "Children?" he calls.

"Here, we're here!" The king steps out of the bushes and offers a royal smile.

"Come out where we can see you," says Tom.

"But we're just right here."

"He really called them that?" says Anne.

"He did."

"I wouldn't," says Tom. "Not out loud."

Dallas nods at Tom's tumbler. "Fuel light's on," he says.

"Fill 'er up," says Tom.

It's a small private lake, owned by some friends of some friends who invited the two families to come and enjoy the dock for the day. The water is black and clean and deep.

"I WON'T EAT THEM," the queen says, crossing her arms.

"But you're the traitor," says the king.

"I'm not."

"Then prove your loyalty."

"Loyalty?"

"That I can trust you."

"Eat them, eat them," the two little boys chant.

"WHAT ABOUT ELAINE?" says Rebecca.

"Elaine?" says Tom. "Elaine from work Elaine?" He plucks an ice cube from his drink and runs it down Rebecca's arm.

"Careful, it's a trap," says Dallas, on his back with his eyes closed. Anne kneads his stomach with her foot.

"Elaine has a boyfriend," Tom says. "Look, goosebumps."

Rebecca shrugs away from the ice. "Babe," she says, "I didn't ask if Elaine had a boyfriend."

"Babe, you didn't ask anything. You said what about Elaine, to which I'm offering something I know: she has a boyfriend."

"Elaine who?" says Dallas. "That would've been the safe thing to say."

"Why do I care if she has a boyfriend or not?" says Rebecca.

"Oh dear," says Anne. "This Elaine is getting too much airtime. Would you all please have a look at this place! Take a second to look around!"

"You could walk on those lily pads," says Tom.

"Anyway," says Rebecca. "Her breasts, they're always out there, sitting on her keyboard like a couple of pigeons."

"Pigeons?" says Dallas. He picks up Anne's foot and begins to crack her toes.

Rebecca wags her finger at Tom. "Don't tell me you guys don't make excuses to ogle those birds."

"Pigeons are filthy," says Tom.

"Ouch!" says Anne.

"What's going on here?" says Rebecca.

"It feels amazing," says Anne. "He'll do yours next, if you want."

"I clip her fingernails too," says Dallas. "I'm in charge of all the family grooming."

"That's more than we need to know," says Rebecca. "Wouldn't you say, Tom?"

"I've heard stranger things," says Tom.

"Like what?" says Rebecca.

"Grooming is pretty standard fare for couples. You used to like it when I brushed your hair."

"That was years ago," says Rebecca.

"You remember, though."

"I have a brush in my purse," offers Anne.

"No," says Rebecca.

"Maybe you'd like Dallas to do it. Or some other guy?" says Tom.

"Don't turn this around," says Rebecca. She tosses the dregs of her drink into the lake. "You're just mad because I mentioned your girlfriend."

"Elaine," says Anne. "This woman."

"There's cheating and there's cheating," says Tom.

"Oh? I only know of one kind," says Rebecca.

"Imagined and real," says Tom.

"No way," says Dallas. "Imagined is okay. My imagination's all mine."

"I'll give you that," says Anne. "You can do whatever you want in there." She taps his forehead with her toes.

"You're the kind of woman who'd kick me out for thinking the wrong thing," says Tom.

"Then what're you still doing here?" says Rebecca.

"Do you want my hat, Rebecca?" says Anne. "This sun. What a day."

"A QUEST," says the king. "If you won't eat the death berries you must go on a quest. Walk until we can't see you anymore."

Arbutus leaves crackle beneath the queen's feet. She flicks her braids and picks at a scab on her arm.

The youngest boy squeaks, "But how will she find her way back?"

"I know where she's going," says the king. "Girls never go far."

"WHERE ARE YOU GOING?" says Tom.

"I want to see what's out there." Rebecca sways down the dock toward the rowboat.

"I'll come with you," says Tom.

"No one's making you."

"Why would I stay here without you to keep things interesting?" Tom catches Rebecca around the waist and scoops her into his arms.

"I keep picturing those wild dogs," says Anne.

"Hmm?" says Dallas, still at her feet.

"I heard that last winter, when the lake was frozen, a pack of dogs chased a deer out onto the ice, but the ice broke and all the animals drowned. It was too deep to fish them out."

"Farewell!" Rebecca shouts, pushing away from the dock with an oar.

Tom waves lazily from his seat at the bow. "Place your bets. Only one of us is coming back alive."

THE GIRL HEARS her parents shouting farewell. Are they calling to her? The path winds up and away from the lake. Through the trees she can see her mother rowing circles, then straightening and heading away from shore. Her father looks to be asleep, or dead, one hand trails in the water. She's never felt so far away from them. She doesn't cry when her scab starts to bleed.

"**DO WE SOUND** like that when we argue?" says Anne.

"I wish you would go to the doctor about that thing," says Dallas.

"Look, they're kissing. In the boat."

"It would probably take five minutes to remove."

"**THEY THINK WE'RE** serious," says Rebecca. "I can tell Anne thinks we're on the rocks for real."

"It's sweet," says Tom, "that she'd care."

"She's so sheltered. Our Sophie's more worldly."

"She's fine."

"Who?"

"Whoever," says Tom. "No more talking."

"All to ourselves," says Rebecca, dropping the oars and letting the boat drift. "I feel like the queen of this place."

THE ELDERBERRIES REMAIN uneaten on their plate of bark.

"Come out, come out wherever you are," calls the king. He hadn't expected her to go so far so fast.

Single file, the children go after her, climb the path away from the lake.

"**THEY'RE TOO QUIET**," says Anne.

"You're right, they look happy out there," says Dallas.

"Children?" Anne calls. "All hands on deck! Five, four, three..."

THE PATH OPENS into a mossy clearing where a cabin once stood. Beams lie criss-crossed and rotting before her. Miraculously, two walls are still standing. Who knows what holds them up? Finders keepers. In the distance the girl hears her parents calling, the boys whining. She scrambles over the remnants of a corrugated tin roof and crouches where the walls meet, where the sun doesn't reach.

"Treason," she says, licking blood from her arm. Not a word she'll easily forget.

Chaperone

Chaperone

HOLT TURNED TWICE beneath a shower nozzle before exiting the change room through a heavy cedar door. Outside, snowflakes fizzled on his skin. To his right, he saw his daughter, Beth, neck-deep in a hot tub, surrounded by classmates. A few feet from the hot tub was a smaller, waterfall-fed pool with a sign that read POLAR BEAR PLUNGE! Beneath the slapping water a dark, muscular man wrung and re-wrung a whip of long black hair.

"Ugh," Beth grunted in Holt's direction. "You look naked."

"Just about," Holt said.

"Your shorts," she said.

Holt looked down at his legs.

"They're beige. Like your skin."

Holt struck a pose, one hand on his hip, the other behind his head, a pin-up girl. He could see the kids assessing the pouchy flesh above his knees. The bristled wings of hair on his shoulders. The brutal scar where he'd had his appendix removed as a child.

"Spare us," Beth said. She turned from Holt and waved as if to shoo him away. Holt returned her gesture, grossly exaggerated, as a younger brother might, but Beth didn't see. She lunged through the frothy water and into the steaming mouth of a cave, the origin of the hot springs. Holt watched her head bob into the darkness, followed by those of the other children who fell into formation behind her.

Holt rose onto his toes to distance himself from the stinging concrete. The Hercules of a man was still preening beneath the icy waterfall. His abdomen was girded with muscle and swashbuckling hoops hung from his nipples. Holt flinched at the thought of a needle piercing the epicentre of so many nerve endings. He hugged his own flabby girth and let out an involuntary yip at the effect of the cold. Then he waded into the larger pool, a not-hot-enough bath, pressing air from his shorts' pockets. In the deep end, Beth's Social Studies teacher, Wanda, and another chaperone, an athletic dad named Barry, were seated on a submerged ledge. As he crouched through the water toward them, Holt surveyed the resort's impressive view of Stamina Lake. From this height, halfway up a mountain, the lake's ice-chunked surface appeared so still, so compliant with the confines of its banks, that Holt had the impression he was looking down on a diorama.

"They behaving in there?" Barry asked when Holt was within earshot. He widened his eyes in the direction of the cave.

"God knows what they're doing," Wanda said. "I don't even want to know. I started teaching when I was twenty-four, and every year they come with a new bag of tricks. Correction: variations on the same old tricks."

"Hold up," Barry said. "Twenty-four? You started teaching last year?"

"Ha ha." Wanda flicked watery fingers in Barry's face. "The kids think I'm prehistoric."

Wanda had a big mouth, lips that seemed to slide all over her face when she spoke. She was captivating and grotesque.

Holt drifted onto the ledge, next to her, leaving a calculated space in between.

"We were just talking about magnet-head," Barry said.

"The girl has a name," Wanda said.

"But you have to admit, magnet-head *is* pretty catchy."

Wanda rolled her eyes. "You're as bad as the kids."

Holt let his legs drift up in front of him and focused on his disembodied toes breaking the surface.

"They'll have to be punished." Wanda turned wearily to Holt. "Barry's already suggested cancelling the rest of these field trips, but I like this. I don't know about you guys, but I'd be marking if I was at home."

"I wasn't thinking," Barry apologized. "Everyone needs to get away. Forget what I said."

A sizzle of red on the inside of Barry's right bicep snagged Holt's gaze.

"That a tattoo?"

"Yeah." Barry lifted his arm from the water and flexed his muscle. A loonie-sized maple leaf tightened across his skin. "Product of Canada, baby."

"Gentlemen, please," Wanda said.

"All right," said Holt. "So what do you propose?"

"Well . . ." Wanda tilted her head back against the concrete lip of the pool and pinched her eyes. A heat-fattened arterial vein ran the length of her neck. Holt watched it throb fitfully, in time with her heart. He and Barry waited for the woman to speak, for her mutant lips to produce a judgment. This waiting. Holt felt as if he were in conference with his wife, Claudette, about Beth. Should they ground her or just shorten her curfew? No television? Take away her cell phone? Holt was tired of discipline. Nothing worked.

"You're a doormat," Claudette had said three months ago when, after rehashing the same problems — slipping grades, ignored chores, pervasive sulkiness — he'd quit offering solutions and lain face down on their bedroom floor in defeat. Claudette ground her socked heel between his shoulder blades.

"She just walks all over you," his wife growled, toes digging into his back muscles, not unlike a massage.

"The dust bunnies down here," Holt groaned.

"So get a goddamn broom." Claudette spurred him in the ribs and left the room.

Holt had remained with his ear to the floor, listening to his wife's footsteps punch down the stairs and into the kitchen below. The suction of the fridge door opening. The thwap of a few bags of produce landing on the countertop. A dull knife drawn from the drawer.

"We all know detentions don't work," Wanda said, opening her eyes. "And besides, that wouldn't be fair because I'm fairly certain some kids are more to blame." She looked conspiratorially at Barry. Holt sensed where they were going.

"Your daughter's a ringleader," Wanda said.

"Beth," said Holt.

"She's got charisma," Barry said. "You know?" He cupped his hands and tossed water over one shoulder, then the other, a gesture, Holt thought, that recalled some sort of ancient bathing ritual performed by old men in the Ganges.

"She *is* outgoing," Holt said.

Wanda snorted. "She's certainly not shy."

"Hey," said Holt. He didn't like her tone.

Wanda lifted herself from the pool to sit on the edge. "It's hot in there," she panted. She gave Barry's shoulder a cautionary pat. "You don't realize how hot."

"Look, H-man," said Barry. "We think Beth had something to do with last night."

"Sure. Maybe," said Holt. "But she couldn't have been the only one."

"I wouldn't exactly call her manipulative..." Wanda said. She shivered dramatically, then laughed. "Phew," she said, "this is cold on my bum." She stood on the submerged ledge, between the two men.

Holt drifted a little; Wanda's thigh was suddenly too close to his face.

"You're serious about this," he said.

Barry shrugged.

Wanda reached up and adjusted the bathing suit strings behind her neck. Her newly shaved underarms, raw and puckered like chicken flesh, struck Holt as utterly vain. "Because it's quite the accusation to make," he continued, shooting them a look he hoped conveyed both warning and disdain. Wanda squinted at him but said nothing. He could tell she thought he was being hyper-defensive, and her coolness, her critical stare, made him wonder if he wasn't acting irrationally. He should have just laughed it off, but it was too late now. Holt tipped his head back into the water and ran his hands through his hair.

THE NIGHT BEFORE it had been Holt's turn to enforce the curfew. He hadn't wanted to. At eleven o'clock he'd already been in bed for an hour, pleasantly sedated — the heat in his room cranked, back-to-back reruns of *Cheers*. For a minute or two, before mobilizing, he lay staring up at the popcorn stucco ceiling and imagined neglecting his duty. What if he just fell asleep? Closed his eyes and indulged his weariness. At this hour, who could blame him? But if something happened to one of the kids, Wanda would blame him. The other parents would blame him. And of course he would blame himself.

Holt pulled the too-small courtesy bathrobe from its hanger in the closet and shoved his bare feet into a pair of snow-soggy shoes. The hotel halls were chilly and dimly lit; each corridor looked the same. On the elevator landing, he paused and tried to remember the way to the kids' rooms. A side table and two wingback chairs were arranged there. On the table, with a few slick travel magazines, there was a potted orchid, its single stem held upright with what looked like skewers. Holt sat, touched the white petals, and wasn't too surprised to find them fake. An elevator arrived and dinged open to reveal no one. Holt wasn't sure if he should be riding the carriage up or down so he didn't move. The doors slid shut and his reflection appeared before him. In the bleary metal he saw a man holding his robe closed at the throat in a manner that resembled a modest housewife who's opened her front door to an unannounced visitor: wary, but curious. He also saw that his legs were crossed, a position Beth often snarked was too feminine for a man. Still, he didn't move.

On the wall above him, a sepia photograph showed the hot springs as they'd looked in the 1920s, before ski lifts had been strung up the mountainside and the resort had been built. Because he couldn't bring himself to stand, to sacrifice the warm patch he'd created on the chair, he strained to read the caption beneath the photo. At the time the picture was taken a mining company had owned the land and had excavated the area's first crude swimming pool for the benefit of its employees. But for hundreds of years before that, the land had been a summer camp, and no doubt a place of spiritual significance, for the natives during their annual huckleberry harvest. Holt liked to think of the place as it had been before the cement was poured and the pool floor painted aquamarine. He liked to imagine a tribe stripping off their baskets and buckskins, and easing into the natural pools. He also liked to imagine the miners inviting their wives or girlfriends up for an innocent swim, those demure women who, in the photograph, wore bathing caps and swimsuits that covered their thighs.

He'd almost forgotten why he was there, on the elevator landing, fingering a fake orchid's petals, but now he could hear muffled laughter and some sort of rhythmic beat, chanting maybe. Had it just begun, or was he only tuning in to it now? Holt rose from the chair and scuffed in the direction of the sound, past an ice machine producing small, internal avalanches, past the open door to a supplies room displaying stacked linens and spray bottles of blue liquid. He felt as though he were navigating a medieval castle; the wall lighting was torch-like, flickering. The chanting, sacrificial. It amplified as he approached the end of the hall. He couldn't be certain (though he was), but his daughter's assured tone sounded like it was leading the refrain: "Mag-net-head, mag-net-head, mag-net-head." Holt put his ear to the door. He heard the congested voices of boys in the throes of puberty, the idiotic twittering of girls who weren't dumb. He heard his heart chugging out of its earlier stupor. Naturally, the door was locked.

"Hey," Holt hissed loudly. "Open up." He rattled the handle before remembering that his room key, one of those credit card types, had been programmed to access all of the kids' rooms. He pulled the card from his robe pocket and slid it into the lock.

What hit him first was the smell. A roomful of kids who didn't yet practise the daily swipe of underarm deodorant, who didn't yet realize the smell was coming from them. He'd taken only one or two strides toward the balcony doors, which he intended to open, when he saw the girl. She was passed out on the floor between the two beds, haloed with crushed beer cans, welts ripening on her forehead. He stopped. A lone, delirious shriek escaped from somewhere behind him. Boys and girls were sprawled across the floor and beds, limbs overlapping. Like a bunch of five-year-olds, pretending to be asleep. Some convulsed with restrained laughter. Holt tried to single out Beth in the dog-pile. He looked for a hand or a foot.

HOLT LIFTED HIS head from the water to find Wanda and Barry still there, waiting him out. Fine. If they wanted to keep on about this, okay then. "Your son's no pushover," Holt said. Barry's kid was a waifish, loud-mouthed boy.

"Whoa," Barry said. "Careful now."

Wanda slipped back into the pool and stood a few feet before the men with her hands on her hips.

"This isn't the Spanish Inquisition," she said, raising one foot from the water and wiggling her toes. "Hey you!" she yelped when Barry grabbed her ankle. "Can't you see I'm doing a leg regime?" She floundered unconvincingly.

Maintaining his grip on Wanda's ankle, Barry said to Holt, "This is about magnet-head and your daughter. Somebody had to get that beer."

"Need I remind you," said Holt, a great surge of blood rushing to his head, "that Beth is fourteen?"

"She has a way with men," Wanda said, "that, as her father, I think you choose not to see."

"Men," said Holt, incredulous, panting. His balance faltered; had he not been supported by water he would have staggered.

"She's tall," Wanda went on. "She puts herself together . . . let's just say, she's more womanly than other girls her age."

What the hell was she talking about? Beth was coltish and breastless. As far as Holt could see, there wasn't anything womanly about her except that, sometimes, he glimpsed bits of Claudette in Beth—her small mouth that revealed very few teeth when she smiled, the sway in her back that was becoming more pronounced with age—but that was it; the extent to which Beth was a woman was apparent only in the way she would one day look like her mother.

"They seduced someone into booting for them," Barry said. "Beth must have convinced some guy."

Some guy, indeed. The resort village had only one liquor store and it was located directly across the street from the hotel. Holt had picked up a case of beer so that he could have a few when he returned to his room after a weary day spent tracking kids on the ski hill. He'd nestled the bottles in a snowdrift on his balcony and was pleased that they'd chilled thoroughly but hadn't frozen.

"Since your daughter doesn't live with you and Claudia—" Wanda said.

"Claudette," Holt said.

"Right," said Wanda. "Isn't it possible you're a little out of touch?"

Holt didn't think so, nor did he think theirs a particularly unusual situation. Beth was taking a break from him and Claudette, living with his older sister, Marcia, a ten-minute drive from their home. Marcia had already been through this kind of thing. Her eldest daughter, now at university, had dropped out of school at fifteen to follow her boyfriend to an ashram, then down to a beach on the Baja. When she fell out of the boyfriend's favour she hitched across two borders, the entire 1-5 home.

"It's fine," Marcia had assured Holt when he phoned to make the arrangements.

"It won't be for long," he promised.

"She's a good kid," Marcia said. "Really, it's fine."

And apparently Beth was good with Marcia, made conversation, did her homework, and emptied the dishwasher without being told.

A murder of crows was flying overhead, though they didn't appear to be flying so much as suspended by fishing line, part of the diorama Holt felt he was in. The mountain on the opposite side of Stamina Lake, which had earlier been obscured by low cloud, now loomed stunningly near. Holt felt he could distinguish each tree from the next, each unique hood of snow.

"It could be your name," Holt said, finally.

"Excuse me?" Wanda said.

"Why the kids think you're old. Wanda. It's from another generation."

Wanda swished her arms through the water. She appeared baffled, blindsided.

"I don't know about that," said Barry. "But I did have a friend whose grandmother's name was Wanda. We spent a week at her house in the country one summer . . . actually, it must have been a farm. There were some cows, I think, and chickens. We ate these perfect little tomatoes right off the vine . . ."

Holt crouched against the pool wall, pushed off and glided as far as he could before he began to sink. Then he continued to propel himself away from Wanda and Barry and toward the hot tub with huge, splashy kicks.

THE HOT TUB was full. Holt gripped the handrail and eased in slowly, pausing on each step to acclimatize to the startling temperature. A young woman shifted onto her boyfriend's lap to make room. Holt nodded thank you and took his seat across from Fabio and, in order to avoid the painful sight of those nipples, closed his eyes and recalled the touted healing properties of the springs. Apparently, the water was mineral rich: calcium, magnesium, sodium, iron. Holt wondered if a person who soaked long enough might be cured of a deficiency, if the anemic or osteoporotic could absorb all that they lacked through their skin.

He opened his eyes and watched the bathers roll their heads from side to side. The heat and effervescence seemed to limber people up; it only made him drowsy. But he'd been tired even before immersing himself, exhausted from the events of last night, the slopes that morning, and now the thought of the four-hour bus ride home. Tonight he'd return to Claudette and Beth wouldn't.

"How is she?" his wife had asked last night when they spoke before bed, before Holt had ventured from his room.

"Seems fine," Holt said. He thumbed the remote and stopped on a channel that showed several negligee-clad women speaking into phones.

"Isn't it time we made her come home?" The connection crackled a bit so Holt knew Claudette was in Beth's room, where the jack on her ancient banana phone was loose.

"We've passed that point," he said. "I don't think we can make her do anything anymore."

"Smartass," Claudette said. "You know what I mean. We could ask her to come home."

The women on the screen tossed their hair. The line swelled with static and fell silent. Holt tried to predict the direction in which their conversation was headed. He couldn't. Within the space of a minute his wife could be charming then cruel, explosive then kind. It was one of the reasons Holt loved her. It was *the* reason. Whatever Claudette felt, she felt it hugely. But he'd seen how her moods had affected Beth. As a child Beth had been confused by Claudette's highs and lows. Now she was just pissed off. It seemed to Holt that his wife and daughter had been at odds most of their lives, but drastically so since Beth had transitioned to high school and started skipping classes to hang out downtown. When Claudette went looking for answers, she'd found du Mauriers and butterscotch-flavoured condoms in Beth's purse. Beth couldn't come up with a good excuse for the cigarettes, but she claimed the school nurse had distributed the condoms. Naturally, Claudette got the nurse on the phone. No flavours or colours, the nurse had confirmed; schools these days dealt only in white latex. Still, Holt believed his daughter when she said she planned to use them as balloons, a hoax for a friend's upcoming birthday party.

A caption flashed at the bottom of the TV screen: These girls want to talk to YOU!

"Is she happy at least?" Claudette asked. "Is she having fun?"

"I don't think she minds that I'm here."

"No," Claudette said. "She likes you."

Holt knew it was true. He couldn't think of one instance when he alone had provoked his daughter's ire.

"Maybe we shouldn't have given her the option," Claudette said. "To leave, I mean. Maybe that was our mistake."

"Your mistake," Holt said without thinking.

"Mine? Please," Claudette laughed. "You think you're just some bystander in this family?"

"Bingo," he said. Whenever Claudette and Beth went at it, threatening, slamming doors, Holt retreated to the sidelines, a referee unable to make a call.

"Fuck," Claudette said softly. "I miss her."

"I know," said Holt. "Me too."

Suddenly he saw that the women on the screen were really girls. He grappled with the remote and killed the power on the TV.

HOLT GREW LIGHT-HEADED and left the hot tub to the hard-core soakers. Wading into the cave, he felt as if he was entering a primeval mouth. Slippery stalactites hung from the roof like tonsils. The calcified walls, ridged and grooved, certainly resembled a palate. He muscled his tongue around the inside of his mouth, pleased at his observation, which he suspected wasn't exactly original.

"Mag-net-head!" someone cheered from deeper inside the cave. It sounded like Barry's kid, but it could have been any of the boys. Laughter ricocheted along the walls. Holt paused in the waist-deep water and turned so that he could see outside. He was mildly claustrophobic, but reminded himself that he couldn't get lost; the tunnel was shaped like a horseshoe, with both entrances off the hot tub, and there would only be a few seconds, as he rounded the bend, when he wouldn't be able to see daylight. He drew in a few full, steamy breaths through his nose. Cleansing breaths, Claudette called them. Across the deck, in the warm pool, Holt thought he could see Wanda lying across Barry's outstretched arms, the way you'd hold a kid you're teaching to swim. They wouldn't report last night's incident if Holt didn't, that was the impression he'd had before he swam away. He foraged deeper into the cave, which was lit solely by murky, underwater beams. There were pockets with natural shelves off the main loop and twice he passed couples knotted up in them. He felt like a spectator at a peep show. This was no place for kids. He thought of the sepia photo hanging at the elevator landing and longed for that muted, gentler time. But there was no going back. Some guy, indeed. Holt had bought the beer for the kids. He'd picked up a flat. Beth had asked him sweetly and he'd made her promise they'd stay in their rooms. It was stupid of him, but he'd thought they might not even drink it, might not like the taste.

Holt sank into the water and crawled forward on his fingertips, with only his head exposed.

"Sssssss," he hissed as he rounded the scoop of the horseshoe.

"What's that?" one of the kids said.

"Sssssss," Holt hissed again.

"A snake," Holt heard Beth say, flatly. He couldn't see her yet.

Last night, he'd identified his daughter amid the rank chaos of the hotel room, huddled on the floor. He hadn't seen her at first because she was cocooned between boys. They'd shed like flimsy skins at his approach.

"Party's over," Holt said, looking down at his daughter. Most of the kids went obediently for the door, but a few girls stayed.

"That's a good look for you," Beth said, referring to his robe and sneakers.

Holt tightened the belt. "Flattery will get you everywhere," he said, trying to play it cool. Beth rolled her eyes. Holt rolled his. Then he turned and knelt to check magnet-head's pulse. He recognized the girl, Mariko was her name. As kids, she and Beth had coordinated weekend sleepovers. Holt even knew that the scar on Mariko's left cheek, crescent-shaped and white, was the tragic mark of a falling food processor blade that, at one time, but never again, had hung on the inside of their pantry door.

"All right," said Holt. "Who's gonna tell me what happened here?"

Mariko groaned and rolled onto her side.

"What does it look like," Beth deadpanned.

Holt picked up a crushed can and tossed it at her. "Were you chucking these at Mariko's head?"

"She's the one who passed out," said a normally shy girl, lippy with intoxication.

Another sputtered, "She's got this, like, magnetic field around her head!"

"I see," said Holt. On the bedside table he counted a few bottles of liquor that he hadn't purchased. Peach schnapps, sambuca, Malibu.

"You gonna tell Mom?" Beth asked.

"Don't know," said Holt. "You?"

"It sort of depends."

"Right," said Holt. He slid his arms beneath Mariko's back and knees and ratcheted her up off the floor. The girl's eyes blurted open and closed.

"Hey," Beth said. "What are you doing?" She scuttled to block Holt's path from the room. "She's fine! It was just a joke. Leave her here!"

But Holt knew he couldn't leave Mariko in his daughter's care. What if they tormented her some more? What if she choked on vomit? He had to take her to Wanda's room.

"Move," said Holt.

Beth stood with her legs triangled before the door.

"As if," she said.

Silently, Holt counted to ten. "Move now," he said. He used Mariko's limp feet to try to nudge his daughter aside, but Beth held her ground. Holt wasn't normally the one to engage in showdowns with his daughter. He realized that, for once, he might be experiencing Claudette's point of view. For no reason, he thought of that old phrase, the lady of the house. It was never "ladies." Maybe Beth would never return home.

"You know," Holt said, "you've really messed up this time."

"Uh, no," Beth said. "That would be you."

"So we're tied," Holt said, the girl growing heavy in his arms. "Now please get the fuck out of my way."

He didn't say it with conviction; he said it with fatigue. Regardless, it had the effect of wiping Beth's face clean of its sneer. Like a damp cloth to sponge food from a baby's mouth. Maybe he hadn't been this close to his daughter for a while, but Beth's features looked large, swollen. It might have been the alcohol, but it was also her age. She was growing into herself. Her nose was too big for her face. Her eyes seemed to open dangerously wide. She looked weird, like an imposter. She stood aside.

Holt manoeuvred Mariko through the doorframe and began down the hall toward the elevator landing, its purgatorial arrangement of table and chairs.

When he knocked, Wanda opened the door only a crack. Then she took in Mariko draped across Holt's arms and swung the door wide. "What the hell?" she said, looking at him, not Mariko, eyes bulging in astonishment.

"It's exactly what it smells like." Mariko reeked of sugary booze. "Can I come in?"

"Oh god, what am I going to tell her parents? The school?"

"Do you want me to get a cot in here?" Holt said as he made his way into the room.

"H-man," Barry said. He was tucked up toward the bed frame where he couldn't be seen from the doorway. A card game was in progress on the duvet.

"Move those, will you?" Holt said, nodding at the deck.

Barry coughed superficially and swiped the cards into his hand. "As you can see, this isn't strip poker."

"None of my business," Holt said. He laid Mariko on the bed.

"Is this an isolated case?" Wanda said.

"I'll handle the rest of them. You just deal with her."

Holt returned to Beth's room with a garbage bag. "Any of you dumb enough to still be here need to go back to your own rooms," he said. The mood had sobered and no one protested. Holt handed the garbage bag to Beth. "Pour everything down the drain and put the empties in here." She wouldn't acknowledge him, but when he came back fifteen minutes later to check on her progress, a full bag of bottles and cans was slumped like a body outside her door.

Now Holt felt dizzy and outside of himself as he swam in among the group of kids. The water wasn't just hot, it was infernal. He longed for the POLAR BEAR PLUNGE! But it wasn't only the shock of the cold he craved. He wanted to experience the pressure of the waterfall itself, that great obliterating gallonage on his skull.

Holt spotted Beth and crawled toward where she sat, no, where she was throned on a rock shelf. What if she never came home?

He knelt before his daughter's long, child's legs.

"Don't worry," Beth said, raising her right hand as if to address her followers. "He's harmless."

Then she looked down at Holt. "What do you want," she said. "I'm right here."

Juvenile

Juvenile

WHEN MIA SPOTS PETE on the ferry, seated in the forward lounge, she shouldn't recognize him—the shaved head, the golf shirt tucked in at the waist. She should glance at him without slowing (god help her, without stopping) and keep moving. She should be on to the next, next, next thing, not pouring toward him like water down a drain.

"Howdy-doody," Mia says.

Pete closes his magazine but doesn't stand to greet her. In fact, he doesn't even say hello. He offers the salutation's diminutive cousin: "Hi." Two letters. Bones on a plate. Mia notes the magazine in his lap, an entertainment weekly, the cover a collage of gowned celebrities. A feverish pink headline asks, Plastic Surgery?

"Funny," Mia says. "I'm always bumping into someone on this thing." She gestures wildly, throws her hand out into the aisle and smacks a kid's bony shoulder. "Sorry, I'm so sorry," she says to the kid, an unshakeable-looking boy buried beneath a black fleece. He shrugs, keeps walking. Mia turns back to Pete. What was she saying? But he offers no encouragement, no prompt. And then the captain is speaking, welcoming passengers aboard BC Ferries and promising whales off the starboard side.

"Well," she says, backing away slowly at first, then hurriedly. She's said too much already. Her right hand pops up to perform a little finger-dance, an idiotic toodle-oo.

PETE IS FLATTERED. It's been ten years but she's still flustered in his presence. His limbs grow warm, barbiturate-heavy. In high school Mia wrote him notes with scented markers and folded the foolscap into a series of triangles and tucks, which was what girls did then, before text messaging. Even now he half-expects her to return and offer him one of her origami declarations, press it into his reluctant palm as if they're between classes, passing in the halls. He rarely read those notes but always granted his friends the pleasure. He liked to watch them scanning for the good bits, the pathetic admissions — that Mia had skipped out on her mother's birthday at a downtown restaurant because he'd said he'd call, that when she noticed his absence in Lit class, she took extra-thorough notes in case he wanted to borrow them — which they read aloud with a mixture of awe and disdain. Mia's devotion elevated Pete in the eyes of his peers. Outwardly they pitied him, she was such a cling-on, they said, but inwardly, he knew, they were jealous. The fact that she was always turning up, that his coldness didn't deter her, was testament to some power he possessed and they did not.

Please come to the upper decks and enjoy our onboard services, a recorded announcement encourages passengers.

Pete returns to his magazine, the cover story featuring an actress's tanned and hefty cleavage. So what if they're fake? He thinks of his last girlfriend, a compact Asian woman with immaculate grooming. Every pore plucked of hair, every nail painted with professional artistry. She was mischievous and giving in bed and, perhaps most attractive of all, she didn't object when he hit on her friends. They'd dated close to a year and the end had only come about because he'd grown itchy for confrontation. Yet even at the party where he'd recklessly shepherded her younger sister into the bathroom, she'd maintained a hostess's anaesthetized calm. Her resignation had reminded him of Mia. The time he buried her in his dirty laundry, two weeks worth of sweaty ginch and rank socks. She'd actually stayed there while he showered. When he returned to dig her out, he found her pretending to be asleep.

Pete shifts in his seat, reaches inside his boxers, and brushes away the sand trapped beneath the waistband, those glorious grains left over from Oyster Beach — the site of the long-weekend party where he downed pills and erected driftwood structures. Where he and his boyhood friend, Josh, danced frantically to severe EDM and patrolled the crowds with arms around one another's shoulders. Even Angie, Josh's fiancée, hadn't managed to stunt Pete's stride. After she marshalled Josh off to their tent, Pete continued, a lone wolf, grinding up against revellers who sometimes ground back.

The curiosity is killing him. Pete sacrifices his window seat and follows Mia down the crowded passageways. Even with the careful distance he maintains between them, he can see she's filled out in ways he would never have predicted. Once a waif of a girl, she's now solid. Her ass is round and strong. She must run, or do yoga. Pliable, he thinks, recalling how he bent her body for his pleasure. She was awkward but always game. As her limbs whip through the crowd ahead of him, the ship's whistle sounds and the boat swings masterfully into Active Pass. On the outside deck, passengers belatedly protect their ears. Mia stops abruptly before one of the aquarium-sized windows as the Gulf Islands loom into view; Pete dips into a stairwell to avoid being seen. He pulls his phone from his pocket and calls Josh. "You'll never believe it," he starts to say, but Angie responds with a snide, "What do you want?" Pete hangs up. What the fuck? She probably checks Josh's email, too. Never, he tells himself, never will that happen to me.

MIA VEERS OFF in the direction she should never have strayed from, toward the cafeteria, located mid-ship. She clips around the slow-moving tourists, a local with intimate knowledge of the ship's amenities, the less-frequented washrooms, the best seats in the house. The engines have begun their throttle out into the Strait of Georgia. As she walks aftward, in the opposite direction of the ship's movement, she feels as if she isn't making headway at all: not exactly a new sensation, but one she hasn't experienced in a while.

"I'm always bumping into people on this thing," Mia says mockingly to herself and cringes. How original. But it's true. Once she inadvertently sat next to her grade six teacher who, sparing no details, told her of the nervous breakdown he'd suffered because of her class. Another time she found herself standing beside her grandmother's estranged sister before a bank of sinks in the washroom. Chance meetings, close encounters, until now they'd elicited only mild surprise, but this time, as she joins the cafeteria line, nausea bubbles up like reflux inside her and her hearing dampens; the din of the food service — the ladle falling back against the steel rim of the clam chowder bucket, the attendants conveying orders to the cooks — grows distant and flattens into two-dimensional natter. Mia slides her tray past the fountain pop and stops before the hot beverage station. What does she need? She plants her hands on the tray, which is still warm from the dishwasher, and tries to really consider this: the even keel of chamomile or the drop-kick of caffeine? The thrill of having Pete in her vicinity, of being able to walk past him, exchange glances and possibly a few words, was once what she'd lived for. As she pulls the tap on the coffee urn she sees the paper cup in her hand shaking.

Pete. The time he convinced her it was okay to have sex wearing a tampon and she'd had to deliver herself to a clinic, into the exceedingly gentle hands of a medical student whose difficulty lay not in dislodging the cotton plug but in fathoming the circumstances that had forced it so far inside her. Pete. Not even bothering to ask how she was when they ran into each other at a party the next night. And here he is on the same boat, possibly remembering the same things. And here is her hand, shaking. Howdy-doody? Without a blip of warning, the world roars back to life. The line of customers behind her is a riot of ill manners. Suddenly she's starving. She craves starch. Mia abandons her tray and backtracks toward the dessert fridge. Standing before the tidily packaged pieces of carrot cake and Nanaimo bars, she's bowled over with yearning. She sets her purse on the steel counter and slides open the zipper's metal teeth. With one hand she reaches inside her purse for her chapstick, with the other she selects a Danish, a glossily preserved apricot at its pastry heart. The two items switch hands. It's not so complicated, a little bit of smoke and mirrors. She presses the balm to her lips, slings the purse across her chest, and moves to claim her abandoned tray with its lone, steaming coffee. She will drink it outside on the upper deck as if she were a tourist, taking in the naturalist's presentation on marine life. Praise the salmon, their iridescent predictability, their homeward thrust. Give me science, she thinks, sweet quantifiable truths. Anything not to dwell on that slippery juvenile version of herself. Except she doesn't really have a choice, that girl's been resurrected.

There she is, slight, underdeveloped for fifteen, wandering the mall on Saturday afternoon with a list, Pete's list. She was an exceptional shoplifter precisely because she didn't look the part: angelic, skin that glowed pinkly in her cheeks and revealed blue veins cross-hatching her temples. She plucked earrings and sunglasses from department store racks without anyone looking askance. *Shoplifters will be Prosecuted!* warned stickers on the change room mirrors, the same mirrors before which Mia hooked herself into promising push-up bras (sometimes two at once), slithered into designer jeans, then shrugged into her own baggy sweats. This was just before alarm-activating security tags, in the days of security guards, of whom there were never enough to police all those bored and covetous girls. Mia capitalized on her childish looks. And she wasn't dumb. Unlike others, she did not flaunt her booty in the mall food court. Nor did she spend a gratuitous amount of time in the change rooms. And she was genuinely polite to the older, wary sales girls. On occasion, she purchased something. A cassette for Pete. A cowrie shell necklace for herself. But the sports jerseys embossed with team logos, she stole. The baseball caps, stole. A Magic 8 Ball, astronaut ice-cream, Sex Wax. Stole, stole, stole.

Mia pushes her tray toward the cashier who announces the total owing. She pulls some change from her pocket and hands it to the girl.

"That's everything?" says the girl, still cupping the change in her palm. She's younger than Mia, smug in her union job and nonregulation eye makeup. She wouldn't, Mia thinks, wouldn't dare.

"Yeah, thanks." Mia lifts her coffee from the tray, leaving it for the girl to deal with.

"Sure about that?" the girl says to Mia's back.

Waiting for her at the condiment bar is a man in a militarily pressed shirt. He jerks his head for her to approach. Mia's insides fall slack. She thinks of the British slang for acute disappointment: gutted. Until now it has always struck her as over the top.

"Go ahead, fix your coffee," says the man.

She tears open a packet of sugar and empties it into the cup.

"I'd let this slide," he says, "but a couple of kids saw you and, well, there's protocol."

Mia sips her coffee and tries to pick out the tattletales. Easy enough: two ponytailed girls huddle against their mother, watching from a distance. She salutes them, raises her coffee in their direction. The mother glares.

PETE LAPS THE upper deck twice before he spots her again in the cafeteria, leaning on the condiment bar in what appears to be a one-sided conversation with one of the ship's workers. Her hair has been swept into a loose bun to reveal what some might call a graceful neck but one that, to Pete, suggests surveillance, all those times it craned in his direction. He watches as Mia hoists her purse onto the bar and extracts a plastic-wrapped item from inside. The man turns it over in his hands as if he expects there to be more to it, and in that moment Pete knows what Mia has done.

IN THE CHIEF Steward's office, Frank hands Mia the Danish. "You must be hungry," he says, drawing out a form with many boxes to be checked and blank spaces to be filled in. Mia has always been curious about the Chief Steward's office. At least once a sailing an unflappable voice broadcasts human carelessness over the loudspeaker: *A set of keys (a camera, a small child, a locket) has been found on deck, to claim them please come to the Chief Steward's office.* Surely some things, though, are never picked up. What treasure must be stored here?

"Are you?" Frank says.

"What?"

"Hungry."

"No."

It's disappointing, really, the office, like any bureaucratic space—desk, computer, filing cabinets—though the walls are stained a warm cherry and there's a showy compass mounted behind the desk.

"You wanted to be caught, is that right?"

"Nobody wants to get caught," Mia says a little too sharply. "Sorry, but I've never bought that theory." She can see the outline of an undershirt beneath Frank's shirt. Men wear undershirts, boys do not. Men are generous, and boys? Boys enlist girls to do their dirty work. While Mia patrolled the Sports Emporium, Pete and Josh waited for her on the granite steps of a cenotaph dedicated to soldiers who'd fought in the First World War. The monument was the focal point of an inner city park that abutted Christ Church Cathedral. The place was shady with chestnut trees. Sour with pigeon shit. A row of mossed tombstones stood like rotten teeth along the north border. Pete nicknamed the park the Dead Zone for the homeless men who loafed—one on each of the four green benches facing the cenotaph—like leisure-stricken princes, shopping carts parked alongside. Occasionally a wedding party wafted out of the church and into the park to pose beneath a chestnut tree's weighty green tiers. The understanding was: if Mia didn't return within an hour she'd been caught.

"I'll need your driver's licence," Frank says.

"You're taking my licence?"

"I just need some information."

Mia hands Frank her wallet. She unwraps the Danish and bites into the dry pastry. God, they were so immature. Even Pete's toes had tasted teenaged. Fungal. They were stubby and sprouted black hairs. He wriggled them forcibly inside her mouth, once slicing her palate with his big toenail.

PETE LINGERS OUTSIDE the Chief Steward's office. It has a counter for receiving people and beyond that an administrative area. Mia is seated with her back to the counter, before a desk. Pete thinks of the last time he saw her: a beach party, the night of their high school graduation. He remembers a massive bonfire, Josh running back and forth across a log through the flames. That night Pete had felt reckless and in love with his peers. Soupy nostalgia warmed his chest and groin. He went looking for Mia and found her squatting behind the stack of logs where girls disappeared to pee. She didn't see him at first—he stood in shadow, on slightly higher ground—and for a moment he simply observed her. She'd done something different with her hair, stabbed it through with pins so that it sat in a fluffy mound on top of her head. She looked defenceless in her crouch, and happy. He remembers the tide was high and all the bloated sea could manage was a continuum of breathless little waves. There was a moon, too, and the wet stones beneath Mia sparkled. She was humming a tune, some perky summer hit even he recognized, and for some reason this infuriated him, it soured his whole mood.

"Pete? Is that you?" Mia said and tried to stand. But before she could hoist her jeans up over her slim hips, he stepped forward, thrust the heel of his hand against her forehead—that broad, sincere forehead—and pushed her down on her ass. Fwump! The song died in her then.

Thinking back, he feels almost bad about it. He can say now, with perspective, that there aren't enough women like Mia. There's a general prudishness about most single women his age. Or is prudishness just something that happens to women as they get older, as they become less obliging? Not since Mia has a woman been quite so indulgent of his whims.

Pete steps up to the reception counter. "Excuse me," he says, drawing the attention of the man behind the desk.

MIA CAN'T BRING HERSELF to turn in her chair, to face him. The apricot is a lump of coagulated sugar sliding down her throat, nearly choking her. The loudspeaker chimes: *Thank you for sailing with BC Ferries. If you are boarding a bus on the ferry, please return to the vehicle deck now.*

"Can I help you?" Frank asks.

When Mia was finally caught, with a pair of slinky basketball shorts tucked into the waist of her jeans, she didn't rat Pete out. Refused to tell the security guard, her parents, the school counsellor, who she was stealing for. Her punishment was a hundred community hours to be served at the Glengarry nursing home. Every day after school for three months she offered tea and digestive biscuits to the Glengarry's residents. She crawled around one end of the common room arranging and rearranging plastic bowling pins for the geriatric to knock down. And what thanks did she get? The last time she'd seen him was at their high school graduation. He'd held her hand down the rickety stairs to the beach at Mile Zero, tightened his grip to help her over the tangle of driftwood and kelp at the bottom. That brief window when wild roses are in bloom, the cliffs knotted with them, their Victorian scent making her near faint with hope. Mia winces now, recalling the peak of her happiness, how later that same night he'd sought her out where she'd disappeared to relieve herself of the apple cider she'd consumed. He'd come looking for her, finally. She was ecstatic, there was no other word for it. Backlit by the moon, she couldn't read the expression on his face but was confident it had changed. All around them, the ocean's ceaseless applause. "Fancy meeting you here," she said coyly, then tried to stand. He was too close, towering over her like some kind of late-night evangelical preacher. Hallelujah! The heel of his hand against her forehead, forcing her down.

The framed map on the wall of the Chief Steward's office charts what appears to be a fairly tricky route through the islands. Mia has always thought of the ship's passage, through broad channels and around glacier-smoothed headlands, as uncomplicated. Until today, her view has always been the same: oceanfront cottages, private beaches, the lives of the charmed. Often the water is the most striking green. Often there are seals basking on Collinson Reef. Sometimes there really are whales. On the outside deck the naturalist tells her audience that to avoid inbreeding an orca will seek out a mate from a pod whose language of clicks and whistles is most varied from its own. Isn't nature brilliant? Isn't it appalling?

PETE ISN'T SURE what he's doing, what he's going to say, but he feels compelled to bail Mia out, or at least soften the blow. The corridor behind him has grown busy with passengers preparing to disembark.

"Is this urgent?" says the man behind the desk.

"It was a dare," Pete blurts. "A stupid dare. I didn't expect her to go through with it. We were just joking around. We dated when we were kids."

Mia doesn't start at the sound of his voice, doesn't even turn in her seat. Pete's face grows hot. The ingratitude. He wants to take it back. Need he remind her of a time when she arranged each footstep to arrive at him?

FRANK LOOKS EXPECTANTLY at Mia. She can see he hopes that what Pete has said is true, that it was just a prank. Somehow this will change everything, put an end to the paperwork, and enable him to offer her a way out. The metallic coffee has made her insides jittery, but outwardly she is still, almost serene. Somewhere, from someone, she heard Pete works in a bank. How appropriate. Miserly. She has since known men generous enough to throw a pillow beneath her hips before moving down between her legs. Mia reaches for the document at Frank's fingertips and signs her name.

"I don't know what he's talking about," she says. Behind Frank, the compass needles settle on their coordinates. She looks him straight in his hopeful eyes and says, "I've never seen that guy before."

Lamb

Lamb

IT WAS TWO-THIRTY, time to pick up the pieces after the lunch-rush—re-stock the bar, bleach the coffee cups, wipe down the salt and pepper shakers, and of course keep Stefano's wineglass full. He and Ivana were the only ones left in the restaurant, sitting where they always sat, at the booth closest the bar. They were a couple of extremes, either glaring silently at one another or arguing in bursts. Sometimes I wondered if they did it for me, if having an audience, albeit small and captive, fuelled their melodrama. I couldn't imagine a couple behaving like that in the privacy of their home. Stefano and Ivana lived together but weren't married, and from what I'd heard this was the root of their quarrels.

"Peter Pan syndrome," Ivana said in her slightly Eastern European accent as I stripped a nearby table of dirty linen. "It's perfectly you." She was painting her nails swimming pool blue, not bothering to look at Stefano when she spoke.

"The little guy in green tights? Yeah, that sounds right."

"You know what it means."

Stefano slapped the tabletop, interrupting Ivana's manicure. "I own this place. I run it."

She held out her hand, blocking Stefano's face, and blew on her nails.

I preferred them when they were being standoffish, playing Sudoku on their phones. After two frantic hours of serving the hurried lawyers and civil servants who made up Athena's lunch-hour clientele, I longed for the quiet that came once the last table had gone and I was free to glide from one task to the next, restoring order just in time for the chaos of the dinner crowd. On occasion, when a late table dared to disturb my napkin-folding—usually tourists who'd strayed from the shops along Government Street—I felt more resentment than was rational. And this particular afternoon, when the door swung open while I stood vacantly buffing cutlery behind the marble fortress of a bar, was no exception. I tossed my rag aside and stalked out to greet the person standing in the entranceway.

PATRICE. One blue eye, one brown. Resumé in one hand, shoe in the other.

"What are the chances?" she said. "The strap literally just broke. Maybe it's a sign."

I stared at the shoe, a black Mary Jane. What kind of sign? When I looked up I couldn't decide which eye to focus on so looked again at the shoe.

"Is the manager in?" she asked.

Beyond Patrice's shoulder, outside, stood a flower-bedecked lamppost. Fort Street was lined with them. Geraniums and petunias struggled in the wind.

"She's on vacation," I said. "But we're not hiring." I'd said these same words yesterday to another hopeful. Each day turned up more of them: girls looking for seasonal work between college semesters. I could relate. I'd been one of them, though younger: I'd started at Athena's in my final year of high school. Now, two years on, I took a kind of mean-spirited pleasure in being curt

76

with these former versions of myself, in standing between them and a paycheque.

"I'll come back in a week or two, in case something changes," Patrice said. "Can I leave this with you?" Usually, once they left, I would cast mocking eyes over their slim resumés, made bulkier by enlarged fonts. I loved the final heading: Interests. As if anyone cared that you knit or surfed or wrote poetry in your spare time.

"I'll pass it on," I said.

"Baby," Stefano called from the back of the restaurant. "Bring her here." Stefano didn't do the hiring. He didn't know when we were short-staffed or over-staffed but he did know a pretty girl. Patrice removed her other shoe. Though it was April, bright and windy, her legs were bare. I wore black tights until June.

I led Patrice through the faux-frescoed dining room, its tavern lighting dim even at midday.

"Who do we have here?" Stefano asked.

"Patrice." She offered her hand to shake. Her arm jangled with a sleeve of multicoloured metal bracelets.

Stefano grasped her fingers and kissed them.

"Okay, wow," she said. "That's quite the greeting."

"I'm European," Stefano shrugged, still holding Patrice's hand.

I watched to see if her cheeks would darken, if she would withdraw her hand, but if any part of her was repulsed or embarrassed it didn't show. Ivana didn't bother to look up, just continued painting the nails on her other hand.

"Baby," Stefano said to me, "do you work tomorrow?" When I nodded, he said to Patrice, "Tomorrow then. Laura will show you around."

I stifled a sigh. I despised training; articulating the menial details of my job was like performing a monologue on the pointlessness of my existence.

"Does he always call you baby?" Patrice asked before she left. "It's standard around here."

She swiped her finger through a little pot of gloss and daubed it over her lips. Head cocked, she was apparently waiting for me to say more. What could I tell her? A year ago Stefano had inherited Athena's and its confusedly Greek and Italian menu from his father, Dimitri. Dimitri called any and every female baby. It didn't bother me. Maybe it was his age, his accent, or the stories he told about herding goats in the Greek countryside, but after a while I didn't hear it anymore. When Dimitri had been my boss, before I'd been promoted to waitress and was still the hostess, standing for hours at a time in the drafty entranceway next to a flaming candelabra, he'd smacked my ass once or twice. But even that had felt harmless, as if he meant only to encourage me. Stefano, however, was thirty-four and born in Canada. There was nothing old-world or excusable about him. And yet he felt entitled to continue in his father's vein, often wrapping his arm around the waists of female staff — though never mine — to better convey a point, and attributing any unfavourable reactions to "that time of the month."

"A black skirt and white blouse," I told Patrice. "We aren't allowed to wear pants."

"Typical chauvinist crap," she said, pursing her shiny lips. "Maybe we can shake things up around here." Her conspiratorial tone unmoored me. I made the mistake of looking at her directly to see what she meant. Her blue eye was flecked with brown as if, in utero, the process of creating a pair had been interrupted, or as if the brown one was engaged in a coup, slowly overtaking the blue. Her nose was long with pinched nostrils, and her mass of brassy curls cut at different lengths hung past

her shoulders. She was no great beauty, but she seemed to believe she was, and I'd read this was sometimes the same thing.
Her focus on me made me squirm. I blushed and turned to
straighten the menus in their basket.

"Tomorrow, then," Patrice said. She cuffed my arm lightly, her
armload of bracelets ringing. I flinched at the intimacy, then
felt prissy for doing so. I also felt wretchedly plain. She swung
barefoot through the door without looking to see if it closed
behind her. I had to wrench it shut against the wind.

I SPENT MORE TIME than usual in front of the mirror the next
morning and even bothered to hook earrings — gold Eiffel Towers
— though my lobes. I entered through the back of the restaurant, punched my time card, and cinched a black apron around
my waist. In the kitchen, one of the many transient cooks who
passed through Athena's was rinsing squid in a colander at
the sink. The rotting ocean smell made me gag.

"I see there's a new gorgeous in town," he said, shutting off
the tap and running a hand through the tubes and tentacles.
Though he was easily my father's age, I was flattered, pleased
that my efforts had been noticed. Then he jerked his head toward the dining room, which was unlit and cluttered with the
silhouettes of chairs that had been flipped up onto the tables by
the night shift so that I, the opener, could sweep and mop first
thing. I couldn't make out Patrice among the shadows.

"She's here already?"

"Oh, honey," he said. "She's here, all right."

I hit the lights in the dining room. Full ashtrays and empty
glasses lined the bar, remnants of last night's closing shift, when
kitchen and floor staff convened to flirt and eat and argue
about which screw-ups were whose fault. I walked through the

restaurant to where the empty cash register hung open — to show thieves there was nothing to steal — and glimpsed Patrice through the French doors that lined the front of the restaurant. She was sitting at one of the outside tables, eating calzone and drinking a glass of beer. A sloppy bun hung off the side of her head. She wore a tight white blouse and a black pencil skirt that strained across her thighs. If I dressed like that, hair falling in my eyes, I'd look careless, dishevelled. But Patrice looked glamorous, voluptuous, as though the fabric were at fault for not sufficiently containing her. I stepped quickly outside, before she could catch me spying.

"Starving," she said through a mouthful.

"We get a free meal on shift," I said, "but the beer. Heather would freak."

"This stuff's practically water," Patrice said, tipping it back.

"She won't have any problem firing you if you're already breaking the rules."

"I don't think I've been officially hired yet. And you haven't told me the rules." She winked, then handed me her dirty plate and gathered her purse up from the ground, quickly checked her phone. "Let's get started," she said, standing. I looked at the plate in my hand. She'd stuck a piece of green chewing gum to the rim. I would have to scrape, or worse, pick it off before dropping the plate into the dish-pit. And Patrice who, according to her resumé, had worked in restaurants since she was thirteen, undoubtedly knew this.

"Paris," she sighed, and flicked one of my Eiffel Towers.

"Oh, well, I've never actually been."

"So sad," she said, pouting.

I felt like a fraud but couldn't very well remove them. Her resumé claimed her last place of employment was a pub in

London. References would be provided upon request. Heather claimed that anyone who didn't list her references up front was hiding something. She didn't even bother to interview those girls.

BUT HEATHER WAS away and Stefano kept offering Patrice shifts, training shifts he called them, though she was certainly no rookie. She could ferry more drinks on her tray than I would ever be able to balance, took orders from large parties without writing anything down, and neutralized the power imbalance between customer and server in a way I hadn't known was possible. She didn't so much take an order as become the charming intermediary between the guests and the kitchen. And the customers loved her. Regulars chatted her up to the point that she had to excuse herself. People I'd served for years asked to sit in her section. And while Patrice sprinted back and forth between the kitchen and dining room, her apron filling with tips, I somehow found myself bussing her tables, doing her dirty work.

"That four-top you just took," I said when finally I'd had enough, "it's in my section."

"Oh, sorry, they flagged me down."

"Sure they did."

"I get on a roll, you know? I sort of thrive on the pace."

It was true, she practically radiated when Athena's was full. I, on the other hand, darted about in a state of near panic and, after particularly busy nights, had a recurring nightmare that my bed, where I was trying to sleep despite patrons' glaring eyes, was located in the middle of the restaurant.

"Also, I have a goal," Patrice confided one night when we were closing together. "I'm saving to get back to London."

"Oh?" I said. There was only one table left, a young couple holding hands across wine-stained linen, their glasses empty, their votive candle spent and guttered long ago. They noticed none of it, least of all me and Patrice, now out of uniform and seated at the bar waiting for them to leave.

"London has history," she said. "People are still digging up coins from the Middle Ages in their backyards." There was also an Argentinean filmmaker who called her his muse. "He begged me not to leave." Her reasons for wanting to return struck me as both fanciful and fair.

"You should come," she said casually.

"Where? To London? What would I do there?"

"Live," Patrice said. "Same thing everyone does." She was wearing jeans, a T-shirt for some band I'd never heard of, her loosely top-knotted hair a scruffy halo, and yet she looked elegant, an aristocrat in disguise. The thought of living with her, of moving through the world as she did, even in her shadow, was thrilling.

I went behind the bar and killed the Gypsy Kings. If that didn't jolt the lovers out of la-la land, I'd turn up the lights.

"Do you know where he lives?" Patrice asked, pushing her glass across the bar for me to refill. I didn't have to ask who she was talking about. Since starting at Athena's she'd become Stefano and Ivana's personal waitress, giving me a break from his shenanigans, she claimed, not seeming to notice that he didn't try any with me. Waiting on them hadn't been a bother; they always ate the same thing so I just called out for it as soon as they sat down. But Patrice treated them as she would any restaurant customer, crouching intimately beside their table, encouraging them to try something different, flirting with them both. It unsettled them, I think, maybe excited them too. When Patrice chided Stefano for not taking Ivana somewhere

else for lunch, somewhere classy like she deserved, Ivana's eyes
lit up. "I like this one," she said. "She can stick around." But all
the while Patrice was reprimanding Stefano, her fingers were
dancing up and down his arm.

I did know where he lived. The summer before, when the
restaurant became officially his, he'd hosted a party for the
staff, roasted an entire lamb in his backyard. I'd gotten drunk
on flaming ouzo shots and had to be sent home, but not before
vomiting up all of the hideously tender flesh I'd consumed into
a spongy clump of lavender.

"Why do you want to know?" I asked.

"Just curious," Patrice said. "Let's drive by, for fun."

She widened her deviant eyes at me and I remembered a
rash of pranks a childhood friend, Serena, and I had played on
neighbours: filling garage padlocks with crazy glue, blasting
a high-powered flashlight onto romantic dinners, pretending
to weep beside freshly dug graves in the cemetery four blocks
from my home. Serena didn't go to my school and therefore
didn't know me as the girl who hid out on the fire exit stairs
at lunch, away from the vicious tournaments of tetherball and
four square, with her head in a book. When I was with Serena
I didn't recognize that girl either.

"Well?" Patrice said.

"We can drive by, but that's it."

"Yay!" She hopped off her bar stool and clapped her hands.
Then she began loudly flipping chairs onto the tables around
the lovebirds.

"Oh god," the girl said, "we're the only ones here!" They were
drunk, but inoffensively so. The girl teetered off to the bathroom.

"It's our six-month anniversary," said the boy, grinning.

Patrice laughed. "You celebrate monthly?"

The boy looked puzzled, unsure if he was being mocked. He unwrapped the mint that came with the bill, held it in one cheek.

"Half a year is a long time," he said.

"You're right, it is," Patrice said, as though awestruck.

The girl returned, bangs dampened, lips re-glazed.

"Thanks *so* much," she gushed to Patrice even though I was their server. "What an amazing meal." They'd shared a Caesar salad and a Mediterranean pizza.

"I'm *so* glad," Patrice said, picking up their boxed leftovers and herding them toward the door. "To another six months."

"You're mocking us," the boy said over his shoulder. Then to his girlfriend: "She's got a bad attitude. We're not coming back."

Patrice laughed again, but coldly. "What a thing to say!" One hand on each of their backs, she gave them a little shove out the door. She set the deadbolt behind them and turned to me. "You over-served them, and I doubt they were even drinking age." It was true, I hadn't checked their ID. I thumbed my keys in my coat pocket and wondered at the meanness that had crept into her voice.

"Why do you care?" I asked.

"I don't. But the powers that be might." She flipped the panel of light switches and we stood in near darkness. Was she threatening me?

"Ugh, come on," she said, as if I'd been holding her up. "Places to go, people to see." Her tone lightened and I found myself feeling relieved, thankful even, to once again be included in an adventure I'd initially opposed.

STEFANO'S HOUSE WAS a solid, nondescript bungalow on a street made remarkable by blossoming cherry trees. Despite the lack of wind, the petals fell, singly then in sudden bursts.

"Do you think she's in there?" Patrice said as we drove past.

"Ivana? She lives with him."

I pulled up to the curb at the end of the block.

"Just one more drive-by," Patrice said.

"This is stupid."

"Okay, then we'll walk past." She sprang from the car, but I kept my hands on the wheel.

"What's the big deal?" she mouthed at me through the windshield. "You're so uptight." She came round and opened the driver's side door. "Do I need to unbuckle you and hold your hand, too?"

Stefano's curtains were open and light blazed from inside. We hurried past, stopping breathless in front of his neighbour's house.

"That's it," I said. "Done." Patrice had linked arms with me not so much in solidarity, I guessed, but so I wouldn't bolt. She tightened her hold.

"What's in his garage will say a lot about him," she said, as if at some point earlier in the evening we'd agreed this was what we were after, a deeper psychological understanding of Stefano.

"I'll tell you what's in there," I said. "A yellow sports car." He'd rolled it out at the party last summer and revved the engine preposterously for his guests.

"Humour me," Patrice said. But would Stefano think it was humorous if he found us lurking around his house? Patrice tugged me down the drive. Almost immediately we tripped a motion sensor light and I was forced to hurry after her, into a gap shaggy with spiderwebs between a cedar hedge and the garage. We were trapped. Patrice peered out to see if the sensor had provoked any curiosity from inside.

"Pervert," she said.

I peeked over her shoulder. Ivana was the one who'd thought to investigate. While she stood at the window, hands making binoculars on the glass to block the interior glare, Stefano came up behind her, mock-thrusting for the amusement of whomever he imagined was trespassing in his yard. Ivana swatted at him, then stepped out of view.

"Guys like that need to be re-educated," Patrice said.

I didn't disagree but there was no changing a guy like Stefano.

"It's none of our business," I said, crossing my arms before my face and pushing through the prickly hedge. Patrice reached in after me and grabbed the hood of my coat, yanking me back.

"What's your problem?" I said.

"That poor woman, putting up with his crap."

"She doesn't have to. She has a choice."

"You're so naïve." I was two years younger than Patrice. Admittedly she was worldlier, but you didn't have to travel to London or wherever to understand the people right in front of you.

I started to leave again, expecting Patrice would follow.

"I'll walk home," she said stiffly, not moving from her post beside the garage. I was on the other side now, alone in a yard checkered with raised beds of black earth. It occurred to me that I didn't know where she lived, not even the neighbourhood. Her address hadn't appeared on her resumé, only a phone number.

THE NEXT COUPLE of times we worked together Patrice was cold. I was cold back. Two could play this game (any girl could), but Patrice played it better. She abandoned clean-up duties mid-task knowing I couldn't bear to leave them undone. At lunch, when we were without a hostess, she left customers waiting at the door, confident I'd drop whatever I was doing to seat them.

She drifted unconcerned among her tables while I scurried in her wake, topping up water glasses, clearing plates. When Stefano and Ivana arrived at the peak of the rush, Patrice was nowhere to be seen so I greeted them and asked if they wanted a drink.

"We'll wait for Patrice," Ivana said. "We don't mind."

But Patrice appeared promptly, bearing a glass of wine, a diet coke, and a Greek salad, which she placed before Ivana.

"No olives, onions, or feta. I know what she likes," she said, dismissing me.

"I could tell you what she likes," Stefano said, pinching Patrice's hip.

"Shut up," Ivana said. "You don't have a clue what women like."

"Table five needs clearing, and ten needs more coffee," Patrice instructed me. I couldn't very well protest in front of my boss. As I cleaned up after her customers, consoling myself by pocketing a far-too-generous tip, I thought again of Serena. We'd quickly grown bored with making crank calls and stealing rides on the back of the Tally-ho, a horse-drawn wagon that carted tourists around our quaint tourist town. Mrs. Delaney was an elderly woman who lived on my block. We cased her house evenings and weekends, finally making two critical discoveries: she kept a key beneath a bucket of clothes pegs, and her adult daughter took her grocery shopping every Saturday morning punctually at ten. Serena and I were crouched and ready, practically vibrating in a patch of woody hydrangeas when at last the car pulled out of the drive. We skittered around back of Mrs. Delaney's house and up her tidy steps, entering a kitchen where the light was lemony and the air thick with the smell of bacon grease. Everything perfect, everything in its place. Figurine of a dairymaid on the sill. Egg-cup collection in a wall-mounted case. We were climbing the stairs toward the bedrooms when I heard the suction of the front door opening, the silence of the house broken like the seal on a jar. I remember my hand on the heavily varnished banister, turning to look over my shoulder, down toward the entranceway, and trying on a look of irritation, as if the grown daughter, not I, were the intruder. It seemed her mother had felt faint so they'd abandoned their shopping and returned to find us in the act of breaking and entering. Our pockets were empty. We hadn't intended to steal anything, Serena tried to explain to the slightly terrified old woman. We just liked the idea of treading through forbidden rooms. Serena and I were grounded, ordered not to see each other for a month, but even when the month ended, and though I waited for a phone call, she didn't seek me out again, choosing instead to tag along with a group of kids known to play truth or dare in Beacon Hill Park.

I HAD THE NIGHT OFF. Patrice called while I was drifting down grocery store aisles, adding random items to my basket, things that once I got home and unpacked wouldn't amount to a single proper meal.

"Want to come over?" she asked. We hadn't spoken directly for nearly a week.

"Hi is usually how these things start," I said. I knew not to expect an apology. Girls, in my experience anyway, never apologized. We either inflicted and endured the requisite torment and continued to be friends, or, as with Serena, we never spoke again.

"You're going to be like that?"

"Over where?" I said. "Your place?"

"I'm at Stefano's. It's a party."

I didn't hear any music or voices in the background.

"Who's there?"

"Just us, and Ivana."

"You sound weird."

"Baby," Patrice said, lowering her voice. "Sometimes you've got to see to believe. Dress up, by the way. It's an occasion."

After dropping off my groceries and changing clothes, I drove to Stefano's street. The first thing I noticed was that the curtains were drawn. I drove past once, twice, trying to convince myself that Patrice had left since we'd talked on the phone. But the third time she appeared between the curtains, waving. She was wearing her work outfit, blouse unbuttoned beyond respectable, even for her. I parked down the street and walked back toward Stefano's, beneath cherry blossom limbs glowing like deep-sea coral. I hesitated on the sidewalk outside the house, hoping for a better indication of what was going on inside. Patrice appeared again, threw up her hands then disappeared. Seconds later she was opening the front door.

"I've been waiting for you," she said, pulling me inside.

There was a fire in the hearth and next to it sat Stefano on a wooden chair, naked except for a pair of satin, leopard-print briefs, hands cuffed behind him.

I backed toward the door.

Patrice grabbed my arm. "Wait," she said. "Don't freak out. We're all adults."

"Christ," Stefano said. "Does she really need to be here?"

"You said it was a party."

I couldn't help noticing the bulge beneath Stefano's satin briefs. I looked away but felt just as uncomfortable looking at Ivana, svelte and sprawled over an armchair in lacy black lingerie, thumbing the pages of *Vogue*.

"I promise it will be educational," Patrice said, sliding her arm around my waist.

Ivana didn't look up from her magazine. She mustered a yawn.

"Me too," Stefano said. "I'm getting bored, baby."

"Careful," Patrice said, her voice suddenly stern. "Show some respect."

"Keep talking," Stefano said. "Keep talking like that and I will."

"This is about us, the women in the room," Patrice went on.

"I don't know," Stefano interjected. "I think of Laura as a girl. Sorry," he said to me.

I shook my head to show I didn't care, it didn't matter, but of course it did. I turned my back on him and, inches from Patrice's face, whispered, "What are we doing here?" I gripped her arms above the elbows but she shook me off, unbuttoned her shirt further, showing off a garish neon bra.

"Striptease?" I said. "For our boss? No thanks."

Patrice sighed, disappointed I wasn't reading her mind.

"No secrets, you two," Stefano said, growing impatient.

"Shut up and wait," Patrice tossed back at him. Then to me: "First you have to get him where you want him. *Then* you have your way."

"Way? What way? What are you talking about?" She arched an eyebrow and spun away from me. "Wait," I said, trying to grab her again, but she was too quick and strutted back to the centre of the room.

"Here she is," Stefano said, "star of the show." He bumped his chair a little away from the hearth. The fire was blazing; flames gnashed at the mesh screen separating them from the carpet, the curtains, the sofa, all that fuel.

Patrice removed her blouse, let it drop to the floor, and because I was standing behind her I saw it, tucked into her bra strap, across her shoulder blade, a sheathed hunting knife.

"Now that's what I'm talking about," Stefano said.

"I thought you'd like this," Patrice said, striking a pose.

I still hadn't removed my coat. I'd stupidly dressed for a party in a shimmery tunic I rarely had the opportunity to wear. I was suffocating beneath the wool, perspiring from every pore.

Stefano's bare haunches pricked with sweat made me think of the lamb turning on the spit. At his party the summer before he'd bragged that he'd started roasting it at dawn, a detail I obsessed over and that had made me feel ill even before the ouzo began to flow.

"You've been very, very bad," Patrice said. "We're here to teach you a lesson." She moved closer to him, nudging the waist of her skirt lower around her hips.

"So let's do it," Stefano said. "Let's go."

Patrice glanced over her shoulder at me with an expression that demanded I step up. But to do what? I gaped back at her, confused, clearly incapable of the task.

Ivana was still engrossed in her magazine, oblivious of the changed mood and Patrice's weapon. How did she figure into this ludicrous plan? Had she and Patrice come up with it earlier? And what was the point? I realized I didn't actually know Patrice, what she was capable of. She hadn't revealed herself to me in any of the ways that women do, bit-by-bit, trading intimacies, small ones at first to see how the other responds. Nor, I suppose, had I given her much to go on either.

Without thinking, I stepped up behind Patrice and withdrew the knife, sheath and all, from beneath her bra strap. Her hand flew back to touch the spot where it had been. "Why'd you do that?" she said, whirling around to face me. That's when I got my first real glimpse of her, and, if I could have, I would have put the knife back. She was livid and I saw that she didn't take betrayal lightly. I also doubted she differentiated between degrees. Again I had difficulty knowing which eye to focus on so instead looked down at the knife in my hand.

"What's this?" Ivana said, her interest finally aroused. Her mouth, like a leaf thrown on fire, curled into a tight smile.

I could turn and leave, walk out the front door without another word, drop the knife down a storm drain on the way to my car. Or I could try to apologize for Patrice's behaviour, make up some story about switched meds and mood swings. But I didn't want to let her down completely.

"The way he flirts with other women," I said, "it's disrespectful."

"Oh, really?" Ivana twisted the *Vogue* into a baton and slapped it against the palm of her hand.

"Wait a second," Stefano said to Patrice. "What were you planning to do with that knife?"

"Don't you see?" she said, ignoring Stefano and quickly adapting to the new order, one in which I'd taken the lead. "You're a victim."

"*I'm* a victim?" Ivana laughed. "I think I'd know—"

"You should be grateful," I said, interrupting her. "We're doing you a favour."

"Precisely," Patrice said, standing shoulder to shoulder with me now. "This," she nodded toward Stefano, "was going to be our gift to you."

He wriggled in his chair, trying to free himself. "You're disturbed," he said to Patrice. "I should have known. And you," he said to me, "you're what, her minion?"

"This amateur theatre is making me ill," Ivana said. She swung her long legs from the armchair, stood, and addressed me. "Your friend, this silly girl, she invites herself over after work. I thought it might be fun so I say okay. But she's acting crazy all night, parading around, all talk talk talk and no fun at all. Thank god you're here. Take her away."

"You deserve to be worshipped," Patrice went on, but her voice lacked conviction. She turned to me for support and once again her eyes threw me, this time because they were unable or unwilling to connect with mine, focused instead on a point beyond my head. It was as if she'd exited the room.

"Worshipped," I said, trying to draw her back. But I couldn't finish that thought, not with any authenticity, because I'd never been worshipped by anyone. I jabbed my elbow into her ribs. Nothing. I resisted the urge to keep talking. There was so much more I could say, so much more I imagined Patrice would want me to say.

Ivana crossed the room and took the sheathed knife from my hand, then began collecting plates, remnants of an earlier part of the evening I'd missed. "Get those, will you?" she said to me on her way to the kitchen, pointing to a bouquet of empty beer bottles on the coffee table. Her turn toward the domestic broke the spell, Patrice's spell. Ivana had called it theatre and she was right. I gathered the bottles and organized them snugly in a box. It was calming, familiar. I might have been behind the bar at Athena's, tidying up after a long night.

The day after our aborted break-in, Serena and I had returned with rags and spray cleaner to scrub out the mud we'd carelessly tracked across Mrs. Delaney's carpets. Serena, in rubber gloves, hummed, unconcerned throughout the whole ordeal, while I scoured away in another corner, full of remorse over what we'd done.

"Someone?" Stefano said. "Anyone?"

I retrieved the key from the mantle and freed him of the cuffs. I imagined Patrice watching me, judging. What would she rather

I do? But when I turned to face her I met no disapproval. Instead she was bent over, fumbling with the buttons on her blouse.

"Get out," Stefano said, and then, almost as an afterthought, "you know you're both fired."

Patrice was already heading for the door. I followed her, feeling awkward and guilty and wishing I could pull a handful of firecrackers out from beneath my coat, a distraction as we made our getaway.

On the threshold Patrice paused a moment, looking out at the blossoming trees, their cotton candy limbs mock-drowning in the wind. "And what should we tell Labour Relations was the cause for our termination?"

"Seriously?" Stefano said. "You were about to slit my jugular."

"Don't exaggerate," Patrice said. "You invited me here. You and Ivana and your twisted little games. What could I say? I need my job." Patrice smiled sweetly. "Two week's pay and a good reference. That's a bargain, in case you're unclear."

"Sick bitch," Stefano said.

"Not nearly sick enough," Patrice said, gliding down the front steps.

WE DROVE IN SILENCE, except for Patrice's occasional directions. I felt giddy, liberated at the thought of never returning to Athena's. I was also slightly afraid, sitting next to a person who carried a hunting knife and who, if things had gone differently, might have used it.

"I have to know," I said. "What was it for?"

"He's an asshole," Patrice said, staring out her window. "I just wanted to scare him." I pulled over where she indicated, in front of a corner store with apartments upstairs. "It was a dull steak knife, Laura, from work. Don't make such a big deal."

"I'm sorry . . ."

She got out and slammed the door. No goodbye, no see you soon. As I drove away, I thought of London — how I'd actually imagined I might go with Patrice, live with her and her Argentinean lover until I got my bearings. She wasn't going back to London, maybe she'd never even been. Of everything, this struck me as the most ludicrous. I knew I'd never see her again, but felt none of the crushing loss I'd suffered when Serena stopped calling on me. Certainly I was naïve, but a person can learn.

Congratulations
& Regrets

Congratulations
& Regrets

I DREW A DEEP BREATH and released a long and faintly bovine moan. Followed the moan with a succession of quick, shallow breaths.

"She's ready to push," Elle, the midwife, said.

This time I cried out, startling the fireman waiting to catch the baby.

"Does she have to do that?" he said. "It's distracting."

"Pay attention," said Elle. "Look what's happening here. Remind her to breathe."

"The blinds," I said. "It's too bright in here."

"Seriously?" the fireman said.

"Huh! Huh! Huh!" I panted. The fireman's brow crumpled with the effort of ignoring me. "Yeah, seriously," I said.

There were seven firemen in the room. They would each have their turn. I'd been self-conscious at first, but once I got going it felt good: the release, all the noise I was entitled to make as the voice of Sophie, the midwifery department's truncated model of a pregnant woman's torso (with the stubby beginnings of thighs). From my position on a high stool beside the gurney, I assessed this particular fireman's hands — I always looked at their hands — and decided his slim fingers were more suited to turning the pages of Victorian novels than the gritty business of saving lives.

"Say something comforting," Elle instructed. "What would you say if this was an actual birth?"

"Zip it, that's what he'd say," one of the onlookers said.

"Charming," I said, and forced the model baby somewhat abruptly through the barrel of Sophie's stomach and down the birth canal. The baby's head was now fully exposed.

"Oh god!" the fireman said.

"What are you doing down there, anyway?" I snapped in my best simulation of a woman in labour. "Don't tell me you haven't done this before!"

Elle's jaw clenched. I was encouraged to provide sound effects, but such admonishments were perhaps taking my role a little too far. I resumed breathing heavily, bearing down.

"Tell her to stop pushing," Elle instructed. "Once the head is out, the shoulders will follow. Put your hands like this. Tell her she's doing an amazing job."

YOU KNOW, M, of all my temp assignments, the one in the mid-wifery department of the Women's and Children's Hospital was my favourite. I wanted the job to be made permanent. I knew nothing about pregnancy, childbirth, postpartum, and despite being a woman to whom such things could conceivably happen, I was, as you know, still at a point in my life when they seemed utterly inconceivable. And yet, I felt privileged being around women in their most liminal state. While I understood that their subdued movements were due mostly to discomfort, I couldn't help seeing their measured steps and the thoughtful way they lowered themselves into chairs as tai chi-esque. I felt calm there, too, M, though it took me a while to get to that point. After you evicted me I collapsed, though not in a bring-your-lunch-and-watch-the-building-implode-by-dynamite sort of way. More quietly than that. A dilapidated barn, roof caving in one moss-heavy beam at a time. I was stunned when, after three years of blissful cohabitation, you announced you wanted to live with Adam, your boyfriend of only eight months.

"What makes you so sure it will last?" you might remember me asking. I was assembling boxes in the living room, tearing packing tape with gusto, allowing its shrieks to be my own. Because you'd done the legwork finding our apartment, I was the one being pushed out.

"People hook up, then shack up," you said. "It's a fairly common trajectory."

Which of course it is, M, but I wonder if now, with some distance, you can see it from my perspective. One morning you were crawling into my bed, nightmare-spooked, and the next you were separating my hair ties from yours.

"Have you considered," I said later that same night when we stood flossing side-by-side before the bathroom mirror, "that eight months isn't even a full-term baby?"

"A baby can be born and thrive at eight months," you said. "It happens every day."

"It's not ideal," I said diplomatically. "There are risks."

"Everything has risks." You flossed violently. Plaque dislodged from between your front teeth and spattered the mirror. I looked at the mole straddling your top lip. You wanted to have it removed but the doctors you consulted said it was impossible to know how it would heal. The scar might be more distracting than the mole itself.

"You should just go for it," I said.

Your eyes brightened. You thought I was giving my blessing. I should have stopped there, but I wasn't ready to be kind. I said, "You should just knife the thing and see what happens."

You fled the bathroom, leaving your used floss on the counter.

"I'm just saying," I called after you. "You seem to be in the mood for taking risks."

OVER THE NEXT couple of weeks I made appointments to view bachelor apartments and basement grottos. All holes. All dank. You didn't even ask how the search was going. You were all business, all out with the old. In a coffee shop, I plucked a tab from a poster advertising a room for rent in a communal house. An hour later I was standing on the porch of a drafty old character mansion with high ceilings and extensive wainscoting. During an informal interview I told Lhasa, the longest-standing tenant, that if she offered me the room my stay would be brief.

"Fine," Lhasa said, crouching to poke the dirt in one of the terracotta pots crowding the veranda. "It's also fine if you decide to stick around. Most of us do."

"I've never lived with strangers before," I explained.

"The room's yours if you want it." She snapped a leaf from one of the plants and chewed it. A lemon scent wafted from her mouth. I'd never imagined myself in a rooming house. I had no bohemian aspirations. I didn't like doing strangers' dishes, let alone seeing their hair in the drain. As you know, M, I have a near-physical revulsion of public pools.

Lhasa spat green gristle from her mouth. She said, "I have other people lined up to see it, but there's stuff I'd rather do." In other words, she didn't necessarily see me as a good fit for the house, she just needed a warm body to pay the rent. This removed some of the pressure to commit long-term.

"Is that lemon balm?" I asked.

"It can heal any number of things," she said.

I pulled out my wallet and wrote six post-dated cheques.

MY ROOM HAD originally been a dining room and its main feature was a built-in buffet with many small, impractical drawers. Of course, you already know this, M, because you and Adam were good enough to help me move the big things — my faux-distressed bed frame, the cramped pine desk I'd had since high school. Can I just say that you were perhaps a little too gleeful when suggesting ways I might arrange the furniture in my new room? To Lhasa you gushed about the neighbourhood, its proximity to bike routes and cheap produce, and I listened with a dull hatred, thinking: this is what a kid feels like when she's being shipped off to boarding school.

The moment I was officially left alone to contemplate my surroundings — once you and Adam had driven off giddily high-fiving each other, or so I imagined — I collapsed into a heap on my mattress. I looked at the bed frame leaning against the wall where you'd left it, all of its interlocking pieces requiring assembly, and wondered, what's the point? Lhasa knocked and without waiting for an answer stuck her head in to offer me a tin of leftover paint. "Might help you claim the space," she said, and no doubt she was right. It would have freshened up the room, rid it of the previous tenant's scent: rodent and cedar shavings, courtesy of a ferret whose nest had perched on the buffet.

"No, really, it's fine," I said, though clearly it wasn't. Not only was the smell feral but the walls were just generally dirty. There were lighter patches where posters once hung.

"It'll be in the basement if you change your mind," Lhasa said, retreating.

When I heard her descending, I jumped up and locked the door.

Surely it was this unwillingness to commit, to *claim the space* as Lhasa put it, that made it impossible for me to settle. In the weeks following, I woke frequently in the night, overwhelmed with displacement. When my alarm bleated, I was already awake, listening to the ablutions of Ryan, one of my housemates who returned home in the early morning. Ryan worked in the film industry and was in the midst of a vampire-focused production that shot mostly at night. As soon as I heard his feet on the stairs, creaking toward his room on the floor above me, I showered and biked to work, gnawing a dry bagel from a bag I kept in my room. You'll understand, M, from the aforementioned nutritionally vacant clod of dough, what a low point this was for me. I'd kept the baking cupboard in our apartment stocked: flaxseed, chia seeds, vanilla beans, coconut sugar, small sacks of heritage flours. I concocted several inedible flops, sure, but I always knew where I'd gone wrong. Sometimes you'd hover around me, trying to record proportions and ingredients; if I whipped up a success, how would I ever recreate it? That's the thing, M, I never wanted to recreate something. It would have felt like going backwards. I did it for the method, the chemistry, that final oven-baked surprise. In fact, those times when I was in the zone, measuring and mixing, were the only times I wished you weren't around. You might have noticed that I began to time my beet-velvet cupcakes and ten-seed loaves for when you weren't home.

Let me ask you this: was I hard to live with? Was I moody? I'm no clean-freak, but I never let dishes pile up and even vacuumed now and then. In my still-boxed-up bedroom, I thought about you a lot. I hadn't left the cable company at that point—it's likely the last place you remember me working—and I thought about you there, too, wondering if you ever imagined me going about my day, donning my headset and pulling on the wrist warmers you knit for me. Or if, during the hours when we normally convened, you felt my absence? Okay, straight up—did you ever miss me? I was so distraught that one morning I forgot my helmet and almost collided with one of the blue equipment vans as it revved through the company parking lot. I shook all day, first with fear, then with the crazy thought that it wasn't all about me—you'd simply fallen in love. Surely people in love still needed friends.

You'll remember that after a month of staying away, I dropped by our old apartment unannounced, though I wasn't so presumptuous as to let myself in with the key still on my chain. I brought fresh-baked bread made entirely with ingredients (admittedly, some expired) sourced from the cupboards of my new home.

"I like what you've done," I said when, after your initial shock at seeing me subsided, you moved aside to let me in. Truthfully I was also in shock: how quickly my presence had been erased. You'd rearranged the living room, bought a sectional couch and a wall-mounted TV. I held out the bread.

"Put it there," you said, pointing to the galley kitchen where I'd happily toiled so recently. I set the heavy loaf on the counter and, because you offered me nothing, I put the kettle on for tea. I took stock of the neat cutlery tray in the drawer, the defrosted freezer, the matching dishware.

"Everything's so organized," I marveled. "Must be Adam's influence."

"Actually we did it together," you said.

Then Adam, lurking at the fringes since I'd arrived, added, "This place needed a serious overhaul."

"Did you perform an exorcism, too?" I asked lightly, opening the baking cupboard to find it stocked with canned tuna and beans. Adam retreated to my old room, now an office, and shut the door.

"And you wonder why he's not a fan," you said from the couch where you sat hugging your knees to your chest.

"The disappearing act's a bit much." It was obvious you weren't going to invite me to sit so I stood awkwardly in the middle of the room.

"Have you met anyone?" you asked, out of nowhere.

What? In the past month? In all the time we'd lived together I hadn't had a boyfriend. I didn't have issues with commitment, with bodies or backgrounds, I just couldn't meet anyone. You knew this. You knew my difficulty with connections, the dance that goes into making one. I could secure eye contact but then didn't know when to look away. I could carry a conversation but after a while I'd realize I was the only one talking. An absurd question, then, to ask. *Had I met anyone?*

"You're so perceptive," I said. "How can you tell?" The kettle began to whine. Out of habit I turned off the gas but didn't bother asking where you'd moved the teapot. I should never have come. As I walked to the door I freed my old keys from their chain, then tossed them on the coffee table.

"I hope you don't think I came to visit," I said, closing the door on a sigh so great you might have been holding it for months. Were you worried I might let myself in some night and never leave? I must've called the elevator, must've walked through the foyer for the last time, but I don't remember any of it. I only remember standing on the sidewalk outside, watching a chainsaw sever limbs from the massive fir that stood between the two buildings across the street. All I could think about were the birds, all the homeless birds.

THE FIREMEN WEREN'T officially graded on their delivery of Sophie's baby—yes, I thought it strange at first too, M, that the birthing model would have a name—but I awarded them unofficial marks. For the respectful handling of Sophie's battered genitalia; for a deep lunge to get a better look at the baby's position; for ignoring the peanut gallery at their backs. After each birth it was necessary to re-lube the baby so as to simulate the slickness of the actual event, and if any of the men—of the two workshops I'd assisted so far, each group comprised only fire*men*—showed any sign of disgust, any squeamishness at all upon receiving the slimy infant, whether for real or for show, I failed them categorically. My slim-fingered novel-reader, for example, received an unremarkable C. He was nervous—who wouldn't be?—but my gripe was that he appeared angry throughout my labour, even after catching the slippery babe in his hands. I think you'd agree, M, that a glowering expression shouldn't be the first a new human sees.

When the participatory portion of the workshop concluded, I tucked the baby back inside Sophie's belly and wheeled the gurney into the kitchen. The midwifery department was an enclave of eight offices, a small, functional kitchen, and a meeting room. It also had a sleeping nook with down pillows and a duvet where a midwife could sleep if she was on call.

I filled the sink and lowered the baby into the soapy, tepid water, then cradled her head in one hand and ran the other over her floppy limbs, feeling for signs of damage, particularly in her armpits. The fireman to whom I was too quick to award top marks (A-) for his composure during a complicated delivery had, upon receiving the baby, grasped her by one arm and spun her overhead. "Touchdown!" he'd cried, tucking her underarm and jogging around the room to a chorus of whoops and applause. "I can do this," he assured Elle. "I've got two kids at home." Thankfully the baby was durable and I detected no injuries. I'd spread a dishtowel on the table and was loosely swaddling her when Elle entered from the hospital's main corridor. With her came the screeching of a real-life infant being pricked in the vaccination clinic across the hall.

"They're not always such goons," she said. "But today's group was depressing." She opened the fridge and took a bottle of Perrier from the case labelled with her name. Elle was captivating, at least I found her so. She was brash and warm, yet her face was inscrutable. I came to understand that a furrowed brow didn't necessarily indicate disapproval. Complete disregard didn't signal contempt. Elle had caught over a thousand babies. She ran the department and was on call three nights a week. She had a lot on her mind and often had to be drawn out of it.

"Our Sophie's a saint," I said, wiping out her insides then slapping a waterlogged dishcloth across her belly. I knew Elle appreciated wit. She leaned against the fridge watching me, critically or impassively I wasn't sure. She was stylishly dressed in high-heeled boots and a belted dress that defined her mannish body: a waist that gave way to hips without warning.

"Poor gal's just about had it," she said, and approached the gurney to prod Sophie's distended belly. "You might look into ordering another. We bought her from a guy in Saskatoon. He uses his wife as the model. I think he makes them in his basement. The invoice should be filed somewhere."

With Elle's eyes still on me I swept crumbs from the counter, emptied the rack of dishes. I wanted to say something that would inspire conversation but my mouth felt full of chalk dust. In the workshop we communicated with arched eyebrows and judgy smiles, but one-on-one I had no idea how to tell her how much I wanted to stay, not be re-posted to another call centre or island of a reception desk, separated from the rest of the staff, a marked outsider. How to express my relief each morning, turning my industrial key in the department door, and seeing the freshly changed wastebaskets and vacuum-tracked carpets? Even though I might have slept fitfully in a house whose radiators shuddered and shed erratic heat throughout the night, here, at the hospital, systems were in place, functioning and predictable.

Elle tossed her empty bottle into the recycling where it clattered to rest among the others. She opened the door to leave and once more the kitchen filled with the sounds of a real-life baby in distress.

"That's creepy," I said.

Elle turned. "What?"

"He makes them in his basement?"

"Right, well, I suppose he has to do it somewhere. And his product is good."

I was angling to bond, however cheaply, with a shared laugh over a man who laboured in what I imagined was a dungeon-like basement among vats of bubbling silicone and moulds of pregnant bellies.

"It's art, in a way," Elle said thoughtfully, and then the door clicked shut behind her.

I wanted to smack myself in the face, M. I was as immature as the firemen. I deserved to be let go, deserved my rooming-house fate and friendless existence. I grabbed a handful of paper towels and patted Sophie's rubbery pink skin dry before wheeling her into the storage closet. Then, I don't know why, I lifted the swaddled baby from the lunch table and stowed her in my bag.

IT WAS LATE when I arrived home—I still had a hard time calling it that. I'd taken to working well past quitting time, until six or six-thirty, then eating a deli-counter dinner and biking circuitously back to the house. On the front porch Lhasa's potted plants were flourishing, climbing and spilling through the balustrade in a great green wave of promise. In my room I pulled the baby from my knapsack. As you know, M, I collected porcelain dolls as a child, the most unfriendly of the doll family, so fragile, so rigid, so prim. What you don't know is that I had ten of them, as well as ten small beds arranged around my room as if it were an orphanage, and I remember the exhausting, self-imposed ritual of tucking each one in at night, singing lullabies, and kissing them on each cheek. This baby, however, embodied none of their petticoat stiffness. She was more like a small animal in her nakedness, the way her supple body responded, either curled in the crook of my arm or dangling before me, my hands in her armpits as if I were examining a puppy.

My room still reeked of ferret. I opened the window, which looked down onto the backyard, and saw Lhasa combing through the garden, weeding and staking, pruning and watering. Did she have a job? She seemed always to be around. When she heard my window creak she looked up and waved. I waved back and quickly ducked out of view. She'd left me alone since I moved in and had only once drawn my attention to the list of shared chores because, she said, she didn't want resentments to develop among the other housemates. In addition to Lhasa and Ryan there were Mason and Simone, a couple who kept separate rooms. They worked in different departments at the same organic grocery store and were always saving toward meditation retreats. I rarely saw them but sometimes I heard chanting coming from their rooms.

I spread a towel on the floor and plugged in my iron. I'd gotten it into my head to look more professional at work. No one had said anything about my attire, but I wanted to look smart, the word my grandmother had used when, in my youth, I dressed up in a stiff white blouse and tartan kilt for a piano recital. I wanted Elle to think I was smart. I dug around in my boxes for a dress I'd bought at a consignment store and then never worn. When I found it, I held it up and remembered you'd borrowed it, M, for one of your early dates with Adam. I turned it inside out and saw you hadn't bothered to wash it afterwards; the armpits were still crusted with the white remnants of your deodorant. I spritzed the dress with water and pressed the underarms until the fabric steamed. Lhasa sang while she worked. I set down the iron, overcome with regret. The dress looked better on you. If I'd let you keep it, would it have made any difference? I closed my window on Lhasa's song and gathered the baby in my arms.

THE NEXT MORNING I cycled to work in my dress, carrying myself with a slightly more professional air. I adjusted my gears to their most difficult setting and rode the whole way standing on my pedals. The resistance felt like penance to which I could attach almost anything. I thought about the baby nestled on my bed inside my locked room. She wasn't needed for another week so there was no rush to return her to Sophie's hollow womb. And curled around her perfect shape the night before, I'd slept better than I had in weeks.

I locked my bike among the fleet of others and drank sweet milky coffee at Tim Hortons in the hospital's main atrium. Young nurses with tight ponytails and no-nonsense earrings huddled at the tables around me. A few sick children for whom much of the hospital existed were scattered about. Slumped in wheelchairs, listlessly staring at murals depicting healthy kids holding balloons, they looked as though they might have impulsively tried to escape only to be stopped by the impartial sliding glass doors.

At my computer I entered the stack of registrations to a conference on caesarean births, then searched out the invoice for Sophie's construction from Wayne's Plastics & Personals. When I called the number I got an answering machine, so left my contact information and Sophie's model number and hung up. After lunch I emailed Elle the specs for three new properties I thought fit her vacation home criteria — wooded lot, ocean views, beach access — located on various Gulf Islands. (She had not given me this task, rather had mentioned her ongoing search offhandedly, and you'll remember, M, I was trying to stand out, make myself indispensable). By four o'clock I'd accomplished so much I felt justified in leaving early. At home I snuggled the baby inside a sling I'd borrowed from the department's bin of freebies for new moms and took her for a walk through the neighbourhood, trying to appear weary and blissful, the way I imagined new moms must feel. Standing in the shade of a rough-barked cedar in a park near my house, I watched children trying to climb up the playground slide. Their mothers' frustration — *No, darling, the slide is for going down* — was, I thought, disproportionate. Why not let them climb up? I jiggled the sling and peered inside at the baby as if assessing her needs. I was making it up as I went, yes, but it felt authentic, not as impossible as I'd once thought.

"Husha, husha," I said gently, as someone passed behind the tree.

"Have you got a baby in there?" It was Lhasa, hefting cloth grocery bags that spewed beet tops and chard. Of course. The park was a shortcut to home.

"It's an exercise, for work," I said.

"Can I see?" She eased her bags to the ground gingerly.

I opened the sling.

Lhasa took a quick breath. "Shouldn't she have a sleeper on?"

"She's a doll," I said. "Does it really matter?"

"Depends on the exercise, I guess. Can I hold her?"

The playground moms were watching us now. Could they tell, even from a distance, that something wasn't right? I turned from the moms and adjusted the baby's weight across my body.

"Maybe when we get home." I started walking, long impatient strides. It took Lhasa to the crosswalk to catch up.

"Sorry if I interrupted something important," she said, panting.

"Nothing I'm going to be tested on," I said.

"I had a baby once." She said this so softly I almost didn't hear for the blood thumping in my ears. "Once. For exactly five days."

I KNOW I should have returned the baby to work, M, to the safety of the storage cupboard, of Sophie's womb, but I didn't. Lhasa wore her around the garden, in the sling, and I continued to sleep deep and undisturbed with her in my arms. We decided on our shared custody wordlessly and the handover took place without argument. Each morning before leaving for work I would set the baby — Fern, I discovered Lhasa had named her from the labels inside the sleepers she now wore — in a metal basin on the porch, home to Lhasa's spade and seed packets. Every evening I would collect her from the same place. At work I felt buoyant and less tongue-tied around Elle. She invited me to eat lunch in her office, which was decorated with artifacts from the places she'd travelled teaching and practising mid-wifery. I almost confided in her, the strange balm of Fern's inanimate company, but I couldn't get around the fact that she was hospital property and I had, if not stolen her, borrowed her without permission. I wanted to tell Elle about Lhasa, too, and her baby of five days, to ask how that sort of thing happened and if Lhasa's connection to the doll was unhealthy. But Elle still hadn't offered me a permanent job and I didn't want to jeopardize my chances. I know what you're thinking, M, that I was growing attached to Elle in the same way I'd been attached to you. You couldn't be more wrong. No disrespect, but I saw a role model in Elle. Her way of being in the world—confident, participatory, necessary—was one I aspired to. And I needed that more than anything, more than I'd needed you.

Rested from my nights with Fern, revitalized by my talks with Elle, I even began baking again. Unpacked my box of grains and flours and finally claimed the shelves I'd been allotted in the old kitchen: fir-floored, light-filled with double porcelain sinks. I baked at night, while the others slept, or, as was the case with Ryan, at work on a movie set. I left horse-hoof-sized cinnamon buns, bars of granola brittle, rustic loaves of red fife bread on the counter for my housemates, always taking care to reserve a portion for Elle. They ate everything, left notes of praise and thanks, even washed the pans and tidied the counters so that my stage would be set when I returned the following night.

I'd planned to make a cake, something decadent yet healthful, for the fireman's workshop the next morning. I'd been too hard on them, not that they knew or cared. The gesture was for me. I arrived home that evening excited at the prospect of making my secret amends, wondering what Elle would say when I rolled in not just with Sophie on her gurney, but with a layered—yes, many-layered!—chocolate reward to be served up at the workshop's end. I dropped my bike around the side of the house and ran up the front steps. I would prop Fern next to the radio and begin with dates, maple syrup, and cacao. But when I stooped to collect her from the metal basin she wasn't there. I called out to Lhasa. She wasn't in the kitchen or the backyard. I climbed the stairs to her room and knocked. No answer. I turned the doorknob, which was glass, the only one like it in the house. I'd imagined her room cluttered with the effects of living there as long as she had, but it was nearly empty. What must have originally been the master bedroom housed only a mattress, several wooden crates filled with clothes, and a baby's high chair.

"Hello?" I said, though clearly I was alone. I reached for the light switch, but even before igniting the antique fixture, my eye was drawn to the small shape propped inside a large cream dish and peering down like a mischievous angel from her cloud. How had Lhasa gotten Fern up there? She'd been placed too intentionally to have been tossed. I would need a ladder to retrieve her, but only Lhasa would know where a ladder might be.

I stacked the wooden crates one on top of the other, all the while feeling as though I was tampering with a crime scene. I didn't want to be caught even though I was only doing what was right, what I should have done days ago. Fern tumbled into my arms and I noticed she was once again naked, stripped of her sleeper. I stuffed her inside my sweater, placed the crates back along the wall, and took another quick look around. A crystal prism hung in the sash window, swaying slightly in the draft. A jar of forsaken pennies on the sill. And one crate, which I'd mistaken for a bedside table, revealed, upon closer inspection, cloth diapers and their protective covers, and an array of sleepers labeled *Fern*.

"Oh," I said, pushing back the silence in the room. "Oh," I said again, and closed the door behind me.

AS I SMUGGLED Fern back to my room a jolt of guilt hammered me in the diaphragm; I struggled to catch my breath. Around midnight I bundled the baby into the borrowed sling and then into my knapsack and cycled to the hospital, letting myself into the department. The curtain on the alcove was drawn which meant the on-call midwife was sleeping, or trying to. I hurried to the storage cupboard and slipped the baby inside Sophie's belly. When I closed the door and turned, I saw the alcove curtain drawn aside and Elle watching me from the daybed with tired though not unkind eyes.

"I'm here—" I started to say.

"It's late," she said. "You shouldn't be."

"Fern. I borrowed her and then I realized."

"Fern?"

I wished Elle would crawl from her bunk and guide me toward the kitchen where we could talk until the sky lightened or her pager sounded, signalling the arrival of a new human. But where to begin? With you, M? With Lhasa? Dark circles pooled beneath Elle's eyes.

"We'll talk tomorrow," she said. And really, what was the point in spreading the jagged pieces of my puzzle before her, in trying to make them fit? I slipped out of the department, the hospital performing its ceaseless humming, thumping, and whirring, all in the name of keeping children alive.

M, YOU ONCE SAID a baby can be born at eight months and thrive. Lhasa's presumably full-term baby hadn't. Why? I never got the chance to ask. I never saw her again. She'd simply left. When I inspected her abandoned things more carefully that night I found, tucked among the baby clothes in the crate, a scroll which, when unfurled, revealed hand and footprints so small they verged on creaturely, a river otter's tracks in wet sand. I heard Ryan come home, his footsteps on the stairs.

"You all right?" he said when he found the door open and me in Lhasa's room. The sleepers and cloth diapers were spread around me on her bed. I'm sure I did not look all right.

"She's gone," I said. "Did she say anything to you?"

"No, nothing." He sat next to me. I leaned into him. It was that easy, M. Whatever swam in his blood and rose through his skin spoke to me instantly. If it was like that for you with Adam, if you could have explained it to me, I might have better understood your sudden single-mindedness. Or I might not have. There were no blankets on Lhasa's bed, only sheets, and after a while we noticed and Ryan dragged in a few from his room.

I slept late the next morning, as if drugged, and arrived to find Elle addressing the fireman's workshop, the relevant materials already distributed, Sophie at her side. I quickly slathered the baby in lube and assumed my position on the stool beside the gurney. Elle didn't break to introduce me, didn't once look my way. When it came time for my part, I found I'd grown self-conscious, unable to labour authentically. After the first two deliveries Elle touched my shoulder and said she could manage alone.

My contract wasn't extended, and I trained my permanent replacement over the space of one morning. Elle was in a meeting when I handed in my keys and identification to security. I considered leaving her a note, but the words and the tone they might take, gratitude or grievance, didn't come. I walked through the atrium toward the exit, past a child spinning himself dizzy on an IV-pole. Rather than waiting to be expelled by the hospital's woolly breath, the antiseptic blasts I used to find so reassuring, I began running for the doors. Elle had done the right thing.

M, I now know this to be true, but honestly, I was soon too busy to even wonder how. Ryan and I moved into Lhasa's room, and my meditating roommates suggested I apply to the bakery in the grocery store where they worked. Soon I was mixing up muffins and bars and loaves patrons came to crave, and restaurants to special order. I thought of you, M, when finally I began writing my recipes down.

I WROTE THIS LETTER, or diary entry, or whatever you want to call the enclosed record addressed to you at a difficult time in my life, one that's now hard for me to recall. I wouldn't even be sending it if not for the creamy envelope that arrived with today's mail: an invitation to yours and Adam's wedding. I'm curious, how did you get this address? Perhaps through my blog? I started it shortly after Ryan and I packed up our laughably few belongings and left the city, wondering why we'd stayed so long. Now I not only bake, but also take photos of my creations and post them on a website alongside ingredient lists and baking instructions. People from all around the world message me with questions I seem to have answers to. Substitute this for that, make it vegan, gluten-free, kid-friendly. I take photos of my yard, my garden, sometimes of my gumbooted feet treading the small paths I've carved between the beds, and most recently of my bakery, currently under construction. If you ever make it out here, you must stop by. Which is my way of saying I'm flattered you thought to invite us, but we really can't get away just now. I'm not declining lightly, M. I would love to swap my last encounter with you for a new one, a happier one. Do you remember the day I returned my keys to your apartment? There was such bitterness between us. Conceivably, though, the bitterness was all mine.

This afternoon, while Fern sleeps, I will prepare an avocado key lime pie in your honour, then sit down to pen these congratulations and regrets, two sentiments I seem to be offering and experiencing more often these days, and no doubt will again when I trudge the gravel road to the mailbox with a squirming bundle against my chest.

New World

New World

NO SEX DRIVE post-baby, body image issues (what the hell happened to her breasts?). It's been three months, or has it been more? Ben would know but Kirby doesn't dare ask. What if he says, *one hundred and twenty-six days and counting*? This isn't the first lull since Oskar's birth nearly two years ago, but it's certainly the longest. And with each day the territory becomes more hostile, a quagmire thrashed through silently by some, seethingly by others. At first Kirby had blamed hormones, taken comfort in a friend's promise that once she quit breast-feeding her libido would return. *Vroom*, she imagined as she threw the ratty nursing bras in the garbage for good. *Vroom*? More like *putt-putt, cough-cough*. A month went by and still she had no trouble keeping her hands to herself. First-world problems, her niece would say. Kirby presses her palms against the chalet's grand windows and imagines the timber frame mansion shifting a trillionth of a degree, just enough to nudge them from their unfortunate axis. Outside, New Year's Eve snow falls in chunky, virginal abundance.

Kirby looks down at her socks, nearly worn through at toe and heel. Who can remember to buy socks? Maybe on the way home they can stop at a mall where she can splurge on that other elasticized essential: underwear. No, wait. No getting ahead of herself, no thoughts of going home yet. She needs to be present, to tackle the task at hand: Ben. She needs to tackle *him*, perhaps where he is right now, hunkered before the massive rock hearth stacking the bones for a fire that will rage for all eternity. It's as good a place as any. Kirby slides out of her socks. Will he laugh? In front of the fireplace is clichéd. And the fire isn't even going yet; they'll be cold. But the alternative, the couch, is leather, its calfy softness sickening if you think about it. What she needs is to *stop* thinking. She hasn't had this much room to contemplate anything since before Oskar's birth — nearly two years she's been on autopilot, a slave to call and response — and now that her mind is free to gallop off in any direction, to chase down every possible scenario for bedding her husband, she finds the range paralyzing.

"Your nose," Ben says.

"My nose?"

"You're flaring your nostrils. What's up?"

"It looks like bubble wrap." Kirby walks over to the hearth and knocks on one of the stones to see if it's real. Of course it is. This is her brother Roderick's place, Mr. Up-and-Coming. She does not mean this derisively. She loves her big brother.

"I can't believe we've never been here before. This place sits empty most of the year." Ben puts a match to the kindling and blows gentle encouragement to the flames.

"We're busy," Kirby says.

"Not that busy. I'd like to come in the summer. Bring my mountain bike."

"I'm sure that can be arranged." Kirby hates the prim edge that has crept into her voice. They are off course, so utterly off course. Gone is any thought of tackling him. She can just see it, a "vacation" during which she chases after Oskar while Ben disappears most of the day, careening down mountainsides. She hates that her mind automatically goes this way, the way of fairness, or lack thereof. Tit for tat. Why can't she get excited about a weekend frolicking in alpine meadows with her son? Picnics and daisy chains. She can read, have a glass of wine while Oskar naps.

Ben reaches out and rubs her leg. Kirby flinches.

"The groceries," she says and escapes to the kitchen.

KIRBY ARRANGES THE food in the fridge then lugs their bags upstairs. Not suitcases but cavernous knapsacks they've had since university. She sets their toothbrushes by the sink in the master bathroom then crumples onto the bed. The luxurious down duvet deflates beneath her like a sigh. Her eyes are heavy; it's only four o'clock. They waited too long to have Oskar, didn't bounce back the way they thought they would, like they did in their twenties after a night of partying. Now they drag their exhaustion around like a second child, fussing over it, regretting it, trying to pass it off on each other. All those years they'd convinced themselves they were too busy for children. Too busy with what? Devouring the latest HBO series, vacationing in warm climates, bankrolling their neighbourhood sushi bar?

Is it too soon to call Maria? Kirby misses Oskar already. She missed him as the car was backing out of the drive. More than that, she *yearns* for him. He doesn't even care they're gone, barely hugged them goodbye.

"No great mystery. She gives him one hundred percent," Ben said one Sunday when Maria came for dinner. Kirby was sulking because Oskar had insisted Maria bathe him. He'd actually shoved Kirby from the bathroom and closed the door.

"Easy on the bubbles," she called over the crashing water.

Ben came up behind her, where she stood before the closed door. "You should be glad," he said gently, "that he's so comfortable with his grandma." He slid his hands inside the waist of Kirby's jeans and pulled her close. The jeans were already tight — from dinner, from life — but with his fingers crammed in there her fat was quantifiable.

"We've got thirty minutes," he said. "Let's . . . you know."

Kirby sucked in her gut and began shuffling away from the bathroom toward the dining table, pulling Ben along behind.

"Are you kidding?" she said. "With your mother here?"

"Not ideal, but it's a new world."

She leaned over to pick at the remainders on and around Oskar's plate. She did this now — wolfed down Cheerios and partially masticated blueberries from beneath his high chair — more as a means of cleaning up than out of hunger. Ben released her and she was immediately sorry. But did he really expect her to dash up to the bedroom for steamy sex while her son and mother-in-law sang "Slippery Fish" one floor beneath them? That had been three months ago, the last advance he'd made until today, only today she'd been receptive. They pawed at each other during the hour-and-a-half drive up to Whistler, kissed at stoplights. One of Ben's hands even slipped beneath her sweater and sought out the structured cup of her bra. She almost felt it. Almost. But now, alone in this Pottery Barn palace with so many surfaces to choose from, the mood they'd been so delicately cultivating has evaporated. They should have just fucked in the car.

KIRBY FINDS BEN lying on his back in plough pose before a raging fire, toes touching the floor behind him, the ridge of his spine visible where his T-shirt has fallen away. She squints, then widens her eyes, squints again. There's a smudginess about him lately. He seems out of focus, less crisp, it doesn't matter at what range.

"Hungry?" Kirby asks. "I could start prepping dinner." It sounds so functional, so unsexy.

Ben says, "I was thinking hot tub."

Of course, like teenagers. Should she put on her bathing suit? There's pleasure in the removal, surely. But what if Ben just wants to soak? His back has been causing him grief lately and he claims he doesn't have time for yoga or swimming. Other parents they know are good at divvying up the childcare, taking turns sleeping in on weekends, escaping to a movie with a friend, but Kirby and Ben aren't good with balance. They're like two baffled kids straddling one side of a seesaw; why can't they achieve liftoff?

"I'll check the temperature." Ben makes for the patio but stops, they both do, when they hear the front door open and voices in the boot room downstairs. Laughter and bags thudding to the floor. Then quiet as the intruders take in Kirby and Ben's things.

"Hello?" one of the intruders calls out.

"Hi?" Kirby calls back. Silence, then feet hurrying up the stairs. Olivia, her niece, followed by Annie.

"Auntie Kirb!" Olivia exclaims and gallops to hug her. Olivia is nineteen and so well-mannered, well-spoken, and well-proportioned that Kirby is, in the darkest pit of her immature self, envious. In her right mind she loves and is proud of Olivia, who has gorgeously sculpted cheekbones and, thanks to the rigours of her cheerleading squad, an athletic build.

"What a surprise!" Kirby says. "Roddy didn't tell us you were coming."

"Ditto," says Annie. Kirby has met Annie before; the girls are tight in that teenage girl way, practically sleeping in each other's arms so that at any hour they can call on the other to support, embellish, or rehash the endlessly fascinating details of their existence.

Olivia looks around. "Where's Oskar?"

"Home," says Ben, "with my mom." He withers into a beefy armchair and Kirby's mind flashes to the spider Oskar accidentally stepped on last week. Its shrivelled state was so unrecognizable that he kept asking where it had gone, and even after Kirby repeatedly pointed to the brown fleck saying, "There, it's right there," he couldn't connect the two and ran off looking for it.

"Oh no," Olivia says. "You're on a date. This is like a getaway for you. Let me call Dad. He has friends up here. Maybe someone's place is free."

Bless her, Kirby thinks, and is surprised to hear herself say: "Don't trouble Roddy. It's New Year's Eve. Besides, we haven't seen you in ages." Is it a lie if everyone instantly knows it to be untrue? Olivia was at Christmas dinner, generously crawling around under the table with Oskar, rubbing up against the guests' legs, the two of them meowing like cats. A mere six days ago. Is Kirby nuts? If Olivia called Roddy he would just whip out his credit card and book the girls a room at a posh hotel in the village, close to the pubs and bars they are no doubt here to carouse through. And yet Kirby keeps coaxing. "We have lots of food and wine."

"We have plans," Annie says.

Ben heaves out of his chair and through the patio doors. He pulls off his T-shirt and drops his pants. It isn't full frontal but the girls snicker and run back downstairs to collect their bags. The steam twists and twirls as he eases into the hot tub. The scene reminds Kirby of an illustration in a book Oskar likes, a bubbling cauldron, a crone hatching a spell. What she wouldn't give for a little sorcery right now. Alchemy. Voodoo. Anything to spare her the inevitable conversation brewing.

AFTER AN HOUR locked in one of the multi-sinked bathrooms the girls appear, shimmery and vanilla-scented. Peacock feathers for earrings. Designer jeans and little cardigans pulled over cleavage-revealing tank tops.

"Ladies," Ben says. He's lined up four shot glasses on the kitchen island and filled them with tequila sourced from a cupboard. The childhood scar on his chin stands out, appears fresh and tender, as it always does when he sweats. He's flushed from the hot tub where Kirby joined him, briefly, in a bathing suit that remained plastered to her body.

"Shouldn't we eat first?" Olivia says.

Annie raises her glass in salute. She and Ben toss one back.

"Te-kill-ya," Kirby says. "No thanks."

"Don't be so lame," Ben says.

This is no recipe for ending their dry spell. This is quite the opposite. Just eyeballing the gold liquid makes her want to pop Tylenol.

"Where's the salt?" asks Olivia. "I'm not doing this without lime."

"Princess," says Ben.

"Nailed it," Annie grumbles. She reaches for Olivia's shot glass but Olivia stops her.

"Easy," she says. "I'm not looking after you tonight."

Annie wrinkles her nose and flips Olivia the finger. "Yeah, you'll be busy looking after someone else." It's code, of course, for a boy, but Kirby lets it slide. She steps up and does her shot, then fires Ben a look—happy?—and braces herself on a granite countertop shot through with geologic veins. Dinner, now, before it's too late. Kirby begins searching out the necessary equipment. The need to get the girls fed before they go out binge drinking has become her most pressing task. A quick pasta, carbohydrates and absorbency. She rams the heel of her hand down onto a clove of garlic. Get them fed and out the door. This unexpected obligation is infuriating. She left her child at home so she wouldn't have obligations, so she could cater to no one but herself and her gasping marriage. Kirby feels the colour rising in her face. Alcohol coupled with rage. The girls perch on bar stools peering into their phones and sending messages to their friends, all of whom are descending on the same bar in the village: the Black Fog. Ben levers the cork from a bottle of wine. No sense of obligation for him, apparently. Big surprise. She could be in her own kitchen trying to get dinner made, the dishes washed, and Oskar's lunch for daycare cut into non-chokeable bits and divided among little containers while Ben surfs Netflix for something to watch once the child is asleep, or is *already* watching something with Oskar in his lap. How many times has she told him: no screen time until two years old?

Easy now. She's done this to herself, to Ben, by insisting the girls stay. He's justifiably mad. A glass of red wine slides onto the counter next to her. Most generous of him. Okay, so they're sorry without saying so. The girls take the wine Ben offers and disappear into the living room. Soon the walls begin to throb with seductive beats and Kirby finds herself feeling grateful for their lively, oblivious presence. Ben disappears too, follows the girls into the living room saying, "Educate me. What's this crap we're listening to?" The bass is infectious. Kirby moves her hips as she glugs olive oil into a saucepan, then adds the garlic, her mind for one blissful moment focused on not letting it burn.

RODDY CALLS AS the girls are hauling on their parkas and fur-lined boots. He apologizes for the mix-up but admits he's happy there are adults on the premises, someone who'll know if Olivia and Annie make it home. Perhaps, if it isn't too much trouble, Kirby and Ben could also walk them *to* the Black Fog, try, subtly, to get a look at whoever they might be meeting there. Kirby could claim she's overeaten and wants to walk off her dinner. How did he know? So, plates abandoned on the table, Kirby and Ben suit up and follow Olivia and Annie down the forested trails toward Whistler Village, the whoops of partygoers ricocheting through the padded silence like the crazed mating calls of abominable snowmen. The girls half-walk-half-run and Kirby remembers that feeling of impatience for the night to begin. She reaches for Ben's hand and he stuffs their interlaced fingers inside his coat pocket.

"Trouble incarnate," he says.

"They're all right," Kirby says.

The way the girls slip and slide and bounce off one another through the darkness makes her sinuses sting.

"I'm drunk," she says.

"We'll dump them and head back." Ben cinches her up close to his side.

They break from the trees into the Village. The snow has stopped and the air holds all the anticipation of a film set primed for action. They stride along the nouveau-cobbled streets with the rest of the merrymakers, past dark storefronts still decorated for Christmas, then the candlelit windows of an upscale restaurant. Behind the glass, shiny-faced patrons raise flutes of bubbly for a camera. Everyone is celebrating. And why shouldn't Kirby, too? She can choose to mend her marriage, be more proactive. Maybe not witchcraft, but there are libido-boosting drugs she can take, there's therapy. Yes, it's time to seek help outside their marriage. The decision is a steel-toed boot rising from her chest.

"Invincible," she says. The girls twirl ahead. Coats undone, arms raised, midriffs exposed. "Do you remember that?"

"I remember you like that," Ben says.

"Impossible."

"You wore perfume and a push-up bra that unclasped at the front."

"Perfume is vile."

She hip-checks him and he play-staggers. She bumps the needle across that track in her head that says therapy and drugs aren't necessary, her libido is just fine, lets it settle on another, a memory set in the trendy dungeon of a restaurant, listening as two university girlfriends concoct a fantasy. Something about a caveman, being thrown over his shoulder and carted off to his cave. Was that it? Her friends practically swooned as they added details to the abduction. Not abduction, they'd vehemently corrected her. Then what? Kirby asked. What else could they be describing? If you don't get it, they said, we can't explain.

Outside the Black Fog stanchions and velvet ropes corral the line of young people awaiting entry. Kirby is glad of the girls' parkas and boots since it looks as though they'll be waiting a while . . . but no, Olivia makes for a separate door, turns to Kirby and Ben and says, "Come for a drink?" as casually as if she's inviting them into her living room. Kirby doesn't confer with Ben about the invitation, just follows Olivia into the club. Is he disappointed? He doesn't actually protest. And anyway, this is good for them, to be out in the world together. Spontaneous. They were that way, once.

THEY EMERGE SOMEWHERE beyond the coat check, on the side-lines of a sunken dance floor packed with bodies. The music is a welcome assault, disabling Kirby's rational mind, blocking all but its electronic pulse entry into her head. Annie sheds her coat and cardigan as if they're made of thorns, can't get them off fast enough. Olivia's phone lights up and she quickly taps out a response. Moments later a guy appears at her side. His face is composed of entirely fortunate features, his hair long, though not bushman long. A row of pearl snap buttons wink down his plaid shirt. A shirt you have only to rip open. He slings an arm around Olivia's shoulder and reaches to shake first Kirby's then Ben's hand.

"Micah," he shouts. "Welcome."

Welcome? Olivia must see the confusion on Kirby's face. "This is his place," she shouts, wrapping an arm around Micah's waist and drawing him closer. "He *owns* it." Kirby nods, speechless. Here she is face-to-face with any parent's worst fear: a hand-some, successful man who is young, yes, but nowhere near Olivia-young. Kirby should be doing something. She should be hatching a plan to separate Olivia from Micah, get her out of here. Micah leans in to consult with Olivia and Annie, then leads them away, a girl on each arm. Ben startles Kirby with a kiss on her ear, then a shrug in the girls' general direction. "What a zoo," he says. "Want something to drink?" They're going to ignore Olivia and Annie for now, he's telling her. Not all night, just for now.

"God, yes, a drink," Kirby says. Maybe this bacchanalia is what they need to light a fire under their marriage bed. She tracks Ben as he makes his way toward the bar. He looks younger in the hectic light, handsome. How jealous she used to be when women hit on him. Dizzy with it. As he moves further away from her through the leagues of glossy heads she feels it again, though to a lesser degree. She doesn't want to be separated from him. What if they can't find each other?

"Wait," she calls, but of course Ben can't hear; there are hordes and decibels between them. Kirby's heart sinks. She feels awkward now, underdressed and standing alone on the periphery with snow melting off her boots.

"We have a room for VIPs." A voice in her ear. It's Micah, toothpick poised in the corner of his mouth.

"I'm waiting for Ben," Kirby says, jerking her chin to where her husband is one of many trying to attract a bartender's attention.

"I'll come back for him. You'll be more comfortable in here." A hallway, door marked Private at the end. He escorts her with a hand at the small of her back and her mind leaps absurdly to her university friends and their abduction fantasies. Is this what they meant? The door opens into a room with its own bar and dance floor. Here is Olivia, here is Annie, grinding among a select group of dancers. Kirby turns in time to see a vault-like door padded with red vinyl close behind her. Ben is on the other side of that door, but Micah has said he will collect him, and he's just handed her the club's signature cocktail, designed by a mixologist in honour of this very evening and crassly named a "Mind-Fuck." She identifies fresh lemon, muddled mint, and an absence of alcohol that can only mean vodka. Even the walls are padded, the whole room asylum-like, and the music is beyond loud: obliterating. Olivia blows Kirby a kiss, then climbs on top of a giant speaker and resumes dancing, gyrating so unselfconsciously that Kirby is awestruck and envious.

"Get up, Auntie Kirb," Olivia shouts, and points to the speaker opposite. Kirby shakes her head, no, but Olivia shouts again, "Come on." Micah nudges her, makes a stirrup of his hands. For a brief moment they are in cahoots, a secret passing between her and a man not her husband. No matter that she isn't even sure what the secret is, only that he seals it with a wink. And what the hell, it's New Year's Eve. No one knows her. No one cares. She places her boot in his laced hands and tries to be quick about it. Still, he wobbles slightly beneath her weight. She slides across the speaker on her stomach, as if gracelessly exiting a pool, and hops to standing. Almost immediately she realizes this isn't where she wants to be, on display, and Olivia, the instigator, has abandoned her, closed her eyes and re-entered her private ecstasy. Micah raises his glass encouragingly but Kirby stands frozen. When was the last time she danced? She tries at first to mimic Olivia but her niece's moves are advanced, slippery. Kirby closes her eyes and sways a little, invites the bass into her bloodstream. She's forgotten what it's like to be in her body, to pay attention to joints and muscles. Her feet aren't merely tools to kick dirty laundry down the stairs, her fingers aren't pinchers to extract crud from a certain small nose. They do these things, yes, but they aren't these things. She needs to remember this, needs to *feel* this when she's in bed with Ben. She opens her eyes to Micah offering up another Mind-Fuck. He is too handsome; she can't look at him directly, just in a shifty, piecemeal way: jaw, brow, cheek. He's being very attentive, isn't he? A little too attentive? She dances harder. Forget that he's Olivia's boyfriend; he's clearly boyfriend to many. On the other speaker Olivia is trying to shrug free of her cardigan. Kirby whips her head back and forth and savours the wind through the sweaty roots of her hair. It doesn't matter she's the oldest person in the club. Just to be part of the mindless revelry. Besides, she's ageless up here. She's fluid and hot and desirable until a hand clamps her ankle. Ben.

"Down," he shouts.

"What? Why? I'm having fun." Kirby tries to kick free of his grasp.

"You're drunk. You're going to hurt yourself."

Again, his vice grip. That's when she very brilliantly slides her foot from her boot. And that's when, in doing so, she topples off the speaker and back into herself. A thirty-six-year-old woman with a paunchy midsection in a wine-stained t-shirt and stretched-out yoga pants. A few dancers rush to help but she brushes them off and rises in a fighting stance. It comes too easily, this fury. There's nothing deep or buried about it. She's an overpacked suitcase, latches ready to spring.

"I'm embarrassing you?"

"I didn't say that. But you're not a kid. Speaker dancing?"

His words are harsh but they don't sound angry. His face, too: indifferent. He's clearly trying to summon the appropriate emotion and can't. Kirby's heart stops. Gone is the smudginess, the lack of focus. She's been so obsessed with her own dissatisfaction, the inequities as she sees them, that she hasn't registered the dull look on Ben's face when he speaks to her lately, or, if she has, she's attributed it to his back trouble, his general exhaustion. The room is reeling. Kirby looks up and sees Olivia, still in her trance, in love with herself. She feels that old twist of jealousy. Only her jealousy isn't directed at Olivia, rather at the woman Ben will fall in love with when he leaves Kirby, the one in whom he'll confide about Kirby's bitterness, her frigidity.

"We'll talk later," he says, guiding Kirby toward an exit before she even has time to put her boot back on.

"I can walk by myself." She hears Oskar: *Do it myself.* She's behaving like a two-year-old and it's exhilarating. She still holds some power, however destructive, and it energizes her. She's read somewhere that two-year-olds are hell-bent on suicide; don't turn your back for a second. And it's true, she feels a similar recklessness as she sets fire to the fuse of her marriage.

"Everything okay here?" Micah has followed them outside to make sure there's no drama. It's his job, after all.

"We're cool," Ben says.

Something's happened to Micah. Stripped of the music and manic lighting, he's less attractive. No, he's not attractive at all. He's vain and arrogant and a little on the short side.

"Go," Kirby says. "We're fine."

"She's cooked," Micah says to Ben as if she's not there. "Gonna hurt tomorrow."

"Excuse me?" Kirby says. She stops tugging at the stubborn zipper on her boot and plants her bare foot on the gritty, salted sidewalk.

"Always happens when moms hit the club," Micah says, again to Ben. "Do you need a cab?"

"We'll walk. But put the girls in one later. I'll be waiting up for them."

Both of them talking as if she doesn't exist.

"Peace," Micah says, and turns to leave.

Peace! As if he's just negotiated some. Such ignorance. As if he has any idea of the roadblocks and embargos ahead. Kirby winds up and brings the heel of her boot down on Micah's back.

"Hey!" he yelps.

Kirby swings again but this time the boot flies from her grasp and into the gutter.

"Get your head checked, lady," Micah says, then ducks inside.

The absurdity of her tantrum is magnified by Ben's calmness, in the measured way he crouches to collect her boot. She looks down at her bare foot to avoid looking anywhere else.

"I need to stop at a store . . ." she begins, but Ben isn't listening, he's walking away. Does he want her to follow? There was a time when she could look at his body and know precisely what he wanted, respond in kind. A time, even, when she could inhabit the stiffness in his shoulders, feel the way he moved through the world, his effort rising from their low bed, the surety of dinner plates balanced along his forearm. She tries now to access the sorrow in his chest, the chin scar that itches inexplicably in the cold. But she can't feel anything, certainly not the weight of her boot in his hand, nor the lightness when, after a few steps, he releases it into the snow.

Desperado

Desperado

YOU ARE BLINDFOLDED, but not in preparation for a child's birthday game or because you're about to be tortured, though you imagine both: pinning the tail on the donkey and a disorientating blow to the head. It's not a blindfold in the traditional sense. With a fingernail you tap the convex shields taped over your eyes. Though the anesthetic hasn't worn off, you take in good faith the doctor's assurance that the corrective surgery was a success and your eyeballs are still there, tucked obediently in their sockets.

When you walked through the waiting room just over an hour ago it was empty, at least a dozen vacant chairs arranged around the perimeter, and the hush surrounding you now — not even the crackle of magazine pages turning — suggests nothing has changed. And yet, despite the many options available, someone chooses to sit next to you. Body heat slops over the arm of your chair and into your lap, churns hefty circles like a cat before settling. You determine the person is a he. In your experience males exude warmth, are often feverish. It's their biological nature to burn, with internalized stress, barefaced lust, basic caloric need.

He smells of antiseptic, infection brought under control, and you rearrange yourself tightly in your chair, clear your throat to indicate your displeasure. Displeasure with him for sitting so close. With yourself for feeling slightly aroused. Desperado, your older brother Wyatt nicknamed you upon learning of your foray into online dating. "A man walks into a clinic," you imagine Wyatt saying, "*any* man walks into a clinic and my sister wants to jump his bones."

"I'm late." Asha's handful of keys clatter onto the reception desk. "Is she done yet? Maddie, I mean, Madeleine . . . Green." A brief silence as the nurse presumably points to where you are sitting. And then Rainey, your three-year-old niece says, "What's on Auntie M's face?"

You reach for the bag at your feet when the body beside you says, as if picking up the thread of a dropped conversation, "It's probably best you can't see the state of the world."

You consider ignoring him, punishing him for his presumptuousness, his proximity. But you like his voice. It speaks to a long-shelved volume of your past, thumbs the brittle pages with care. For the first time in a long time your heart rustles, a veal calf in its hutch.

"It's not what you think," you say. In less than twenty-four hours you'll be able to see with as much accuracy as Superman, but Asha stops you explaining.

"You should see yourself," she says, flip-flops smacking toward you. You hear Rainey whimpering: "Auntie M, take those off." Why isn't she at daycare?

"Stop," you say. It's a crazy impulse, but you want to give him your phone number. You open your purse and feel around for a napkin or receipt to write on. You don't have to wear the shields, they're to prevent you from accidentally rubbing out your newly corrected sight while sleeping, but once the doctor demonstrated how to wear them, you chose to remain in semi-darkness. You weren't ready for the sharp edges in the room.

"I could just—" he says. "Wait, I have my phone." He brings himself up and stands in front of you. How do you know he's offering his hand? You just do.

"Right. Of course," you say, accepting his warm palm in yours, his other arm lifting you up. As you recite the digits of your phone number you blush, as if divulging the colour of your underwear.

"It's a date?" he says.

"I don't know about *that*," you say, your face burning now.

For a second you wonder if Wyatt has set you up, if you're the spectacle on one of those prank TV shows. You half-expect laugh tracks or applause, but the room remains silent, save for the tacky sound of some apparatus wheeling across the floor. Asha takes hold of your elbow and muscles you from the room.

"Easy," you say.

"I can't see you," Rainey sputters. "Where are you?"

"Don't worry, I'm here," you say. You look back over your shoulder and see only blackness.

"Bye for now," the voice says.

Asha jerks you to a halt before the elevators. "What was that?"

"You pushed the button!" Rainey screams. "I wanted to be first."

"Shouldn't she be at daycare?" you say.

"An outbreak," Asha says, "everyone sent home."

"Contagious?" you ask as the elevator doors decompress.

"You've got bigger problems." Inside the elevator she releases your arm. "Here, you can push this button," she says to Rainey.

You grope about for the handrail. Doesn't every elevator have one?

"I guess you couldn't see his ring," Asha says.

You grab onto her again as the elevator begins its descent. Asha is Wyatt's wife, but she was your best friend first.

ASHA HAS ERRANDS, so, while she fulfils her list at London Drugs, you remove the shields from your eyes and try on sunglasses with Rainey.

"Sweetie," you say, peering over the top of a pair of cat-eye shades, "that man I was talking to at the doctor's office, what did he look like?"

"I don't like those ones," Rainey grumbles.

"No, me neither." And it really doesn't matter; you've concocted his age, appearance, manner, all from the timbre of his voice. "Here, try these." You pop a pair of aviator lenses onto her pinched face.

She pulls them off and throws them to the floor. "Your eyes are bleeding."

"Bloodshot, not bleeding."

"I want my mom."

You're about to start combing the aisles for Asha when your phone rings. It's him saying he wants to see you. Are you up for it? Your stomach somersaults; you're running up the down escalator; you're fourteen, sipping lemon gin in the bathroom at the White Eagle Hall. You'd forgotten what it was like to feel this dementedly happy. You pass Rainey a pair of bright red frames to keep her occupied, then a pair of tinted glasses protectors, the kind old people wear. Each pair ends up on the floor. Why not right now? You suggest the Muffin Stop across from the drugstore. Flirty banter has never been your forté — you are a literal thinker, slow to catch innuendo — even so, you tell him he'd better be a sight for sore eyes. When you hang up, Asha is shaking her head, jamming glasses back onto the rack.

"What?" you say. "Why not?"

"The ring. On that very significant finger. You don't know anything about him."

"Everyone starts out a stranger." You place your hand on Rainey's forehead. "She has a fever."

Asha holds up a bottle of cherry flavoured Tylenol. "Why do you think we're here?"

"I'm meeting him in a public place," you say. "Go home. I'll call you later." This suits Asha. Rainey has just snapped the arm from a pair of sunglasses. Asha tucks them behind bottles of sunscreen then lifts her daughter into her arms.

"Call me if things get weird," she says.

"Aren't you going to give me a hint? Tell me what he looks like?"

She gives you a look that says *tragic*, but whether with regard to you or him, you're unsure.

AT MUFFIN STOP you choose blueberry, tried and true. Outside, next to the bike rack, a woman scolds her three-legged dog, which looks more like a wolf; its coat is the nicotine-stained white of Arctic animals. The wolf-dog stands on hind legs and rests its sole front paw on the woman's shoulder. Snout to snout, they are roughly the same height. She wags a finger in the dog's face and it howls its defence.

You sink a wad of muffin into your mouth as a guy on a skateboard slides past the windows with his back to you. He startles the woman and dog from their argument when he throws a foot onto the pavement, flips the board into his hand. The underside flaunts a naked woman with Medusa hair. Classy, you think. The door jingles upon opening. Skateboard guy heads straight for you. You try to take him in, take him or leave him before he reaches you. His hair is black, streaked with white, and he wears it in a loose ponytail at the nape of his neck. Baggy cargo shorts hang below his knees. A chain loops from his right pocket. A man-boy. Terrific. Now you understand Asha's parting look.

"Jackie O," he says, remarking on your just-purchased drugstore shades. "I'm Dylan."

"Oh . . ." you say.

"I'm going to sit down," he says, as if you're a woman on the edge and he's a cop trained in pacification. "Now I'm going to ask your name."

A real charmer, this Dylan. He buys you a second coffee, compliments the boomerang sweep of your collarbones. No sign of a ring.

"So," he says. "What to do?"

You furrow your brow, pretend to deliberate. Behind your sunglasses your eyes water and burn. You sit on your hands to keep from rubbing them.

"There are several ways to go about this," he says.

"Really?" you say. "You've done this before?"

"Not this, exactly."

There are only two ways that you can see. Stop/Go. Yes/No. It's so hard to meet men in this insular town. You bumble about for perspective. Desperado. Is Wyatt right about you?

Dylan pushes his chair back from the table and opens his arms wide. A fiercely white bandage runs elbow to armpit. Outside, at the bike rack, the woman feeds her wolf-dog a handful of muffin and whispers in its perked ear. They butt heads affectionately.

"Come," he says, arms still wide, inviting.

Is he really suggesting you sit on his lap? You reach across the table to touch the bandage instead.

"Stitches," he says. "Twenty-two."

"Reckless," you say.

"Clumsy."

"Careless?"

"No, never careless."

You retreat into some distant nook of your brain and try again for perspective. His eye contact is unflinching. His feet rest on his skateboard beneath the table. Skateboards make you nostalgic, never a good thing.

YOU'VE SAID YES to several online requests for your company. There have been a few good men, a few bad. More, in any case, than if you'd kept hoping for a fated collision of grocery carts in Thrifty Foods. There was, for example, the lab technician who had night sweats like flash floods. You were always washing your sheets. After a month of sleepovers, he began questioning your commitment when you kept forgetting to cut him a key.

Wyatt laughed at you for even considering it. "You don't like him. Why do you need me to point this out?"

"He's right," Asha said. "You clearly don't want to give this guy a key."

Then there was Sina, five years younger than you and full of hope. He built inner city gardens. The string of vegetable plots along the decommissioned railroad tracks near your condo was one of his greatest achievements. His arms were thick from hours of honest toil, and his green eyes shone with a naïve vacancy you wanted focused on you, always. Sina occupied an entire summer. You often picnicked along the tracks, on precarious driftwood furniture constructed by the idealistic gardeners. One evening he all but undressed you beside a thicket of raspberry canes while you stood eating from them. You watched the dining room in the old folks' home across the street fill with walkers while Sina's fingers entered you. There was a supermoon that night. You felt like a goddess to all men. In the fall an earnest, manure-shovelling woman stole his attentions. You couldn't blame him: so young, so like a honeybee.

Those were the good ones, the bad ones not worth remembering. Still, weren't even they better than no one?

"It's how people today meet," you schooled Wyatt and Asha. You sat in front of your laptop while they looked over your shoulder, approving and disapproving of your online suitors. "The way you two got together is so old-fashioned."

"Looks like too much work," Asha said.

"That's because you're not motivated."

"What does that mean?"

"You just want to hear me say it."

"What?"

"You never had to work for it. You always had your pick."

"And she picked me," Wyatt said. "Beautiful *and* smart."

"If it weren't for me," you said, "Rainey wouldn't exist. This house wouldn't exist. I deserve a little thanks."

"We're forever in your debt," Asha said, laying a wet kiss on your cheek.

"I keep telling you, there are single guys in my hockey league," Wyatt said.

"I'm done with jocks," you said.

"You're too picky. The guy you're looking for doesn't exist."

DYLAN WALKS YOU to the bus stop. You have no idea why you're taking the bus when you could, and probably should, call a cab. As teenagers, you and Asha took the bus every day. So much in your social world happened while jolting between stops. The dance to stand beside your crush without being too obvious.

The possibility that your crush might not move away when you stood next to him, that maybe he liked you, too. You and Asha would dissect each stance and position on the phone at night. Who knows what the boys did, but if Wyatt's basketball-dunking, fridge-foraging behaviour was any indication, it wasn't that.

The bus is barrelling up to the curb and Dylan leans in so that you think he might kiss you but, at the last second, his face dips downward, into your neck. He inhales deeply and you shiver. The bus doors open and close in this space of time.

"Wait," you call to the driver and knock on the glass. The doors reopen and she waves you on. As the bus pulls away you're still shivering. You know him from somewhere, recognize him, at least. Maybe you watched him cliff-jumping at the lake one summer, maybe he pumped gas into your first car, served you and Asha drinks in a bar. That's often the way in a small hometown. You've trained yourself not to be rattled by it, nor to search too deeply for the tether that links your past to another's. In your monk's cell of a condo you sleep for twelve hours.

THE NEXT DAY, Saturday, you arrive at Asha and Wyatt's in time for pancakes. Always Saturday, always at ten. When you enter the house you don't smell coffee, let alone Asha's signature orange zest.

"Sorry, forgot to call," she says. "We were at the hospital all night."

Rainey is snoring in a nest of blankets on the couch. Wyatt's asleep upstairs.

"What happened?" you ask.

"The daycare plague. She's fine now. Her fever broke. But her face was turning purple. I thought she couldn't breathe. Now she has this barking cough."

Asha starts hauling laundry from the washer and dumping it into a basket. "Your guy, the weirdo," she says, pausing before heading outside to the clothesline, "I think I know him from somewhere. Can't place him yet, but it'll come to me."

"Dangerous territory," you say, following her. "Maybe we don't want to know."

"I'm pregnant, by the way," Asha says.

"But I don't even have *one* yet."

"I've always wanted two."

You slump into an Adirondack chair. "Congratulations, really. You're such an adult. What happened to me?"

"You had all this stuff growing up," Asha says. "Family, house, garden." She pegs your brother's underwear to the line and sends it out over the blackberries. "I didn't, so now it's my turn."

"Do you like these sunglasses?" you ask.

"A bit big for your face."

An indignant voice calls, "I want my mommy."

"Can I go to her?" you ask.

"Wash your hands afterwards," Asha says.

You read Rainey stories and feed her frozen blueberries until she falls asleep in your arms. You kiss her cheeks and ears and neck, then squirm out of her grasp to check your phone for the coordinates Dylan's texted to you.

"I can't believe you're taking him out to Dad's old hovel," Asha says. "If I don't hear from you in a few hours I'm sending Wyatt after you. Embarrassing for everyone so just remember that while you're doing whatever it is you plan to do out there."

"Thank you for caring," you say. "And I'm happy for you, I really am." You think of Asha's swollen face and body those first months after Rainey was born. Asha weeping while Wyatt held the baby firm against his chest and hurled himself back and forth in the rocking chair, the only thing that would soothe Rainey. They've clearly forgotten, and who are you to remind them, especially now?

You pull up in front of a stucco box set at the back of a deep lawn plugged with dandelions. No woman comes to the door, no sign of children. Dylan leaps shirtless down the stairs and you can't help noticing he doesn't lock the door behind him. Maybe it locks automatically, or maybe someone else is home. You also can't help noticing his body. Fit but not overly, maybe even effortlessly. Slight love handles hold up his cargo shorts. The rack on which his skin hangs, his very bones please you. When he slaps his hand on your thigh and leaves it there for a moment, the warmth from his fingers spreads across your skin like a brushfire.

"Get out," you say.

"What?"

"That came out wrong. Can you please drive? My eyes need a rest."

They're fragile, leaky in the sunlight. You crack them only to offer directions. Traffic is lurching, stagnant with day trippers heading out toward a chain of lakes on the city's edge. You catch a whiff of the food you packed: roasted asparagus, quinoa salad, chopped peaches tossed with fresh mint. You worry your picnic might appear too keen, too planned. Desperado.

You're taking him past the cliff-jumping lake, past the nudist lake, down a dirt road to a piece of property that Asha's father used to own but that now belongs to her. Forested, rocky, with a trailer set on blocks, it's not worth much, but it's a place where you and Asha spent time as girls. Tanning on the roof of the trailer while ravens yapped overhead. Sipping Coke with lime, flipping back to front, and listening to Asha's father and his latest girlfriend cook lunch inside. His courtships always involved the preparation of many-coursed meals, despite the limited facilities: hot plate, toaster oven, one square foot of counter space. In this corner of the forest you ate heaps of caprese salad, sucked back gazpacho as if it were a smoothie.

"Did you miss me?" Dylan asks, drumming the wheel at the last stoplight before the turnoff into the forest.

"I thought about you. How's that?"

"After today you'll pine for me when I'm not around."

You can't think of a decent retort. You think, in fact, he may be right.

"I know where we're going," he says.

"Impossible."

"There's a dead-end road. I bet kids still come out here."

The summer you and Asha were fourteen you stayed at the trailer for two weeks. It felt like a glorious eternity. You left the woods only a couple of times, with Asha's father, for groceries. Each time, merging from the gravel road onto the highway's blacktop felt like crossing into another land, one where you no longer belonged. You and Asha wandered the bright grocery store aisles in all their excess, stunned. At the checkout, you heaped Twizzlers and Junior Mints and teen magazines onto the conveyor belt, anxious to return to your own private world, which had begun to reveal unexpected intrigue. Teenagers were converging down where the road dead-ended. Evenings, their shouts and laughter volleyed through the dusk to where you sat swatting at mosquitoes, playing Scrabble in the light of coloured lanterns strung around the trailer.

"Those hormonal idiots are going to burn the forest down," Asha's father said. There was a province-wide fire ban, but even so you could smell a bonfire nearby.

That was the summer you and Asha began to crave independence, and sleeping outside the trailer in a tent satisfied your need. After her father went to bed, you stayed awake into the small hours listening to the thump of music through the trees. Cross-legged on top of your sleeping bags, you played hand after hand of Crazy Eights until one night Asha threw down her cards, reached for the tent zipper, and said, "We might as well take a look."

It hadn't occurred to you, but yes, of course you should spy. Without realizing it, you'd been practising for this moment since you'd first arrived in the woods. Afternoons, when the heat became too intense to tan, you and Asha went exploring, followed deer trails to the edge of the suburbs and the condemned RCMP shooting range, the land so toxic with lead it could be used for nothing else. If you roamed in the opposite direction, Douglas fir gave way to hydro towers. When the sun finally set, you had no need of flashlights. Your feet already knew where the land dipped and turned.

The bonfire grew brighter as you approached. You pressed yourselves against a mossy knoll where you could see but not be seen, and communicated with hand squeezes. There were derelict sofas and armchairs set around the fire, bikes stacked four deep against tree trunks. Teenagers not much older than you and Asha drank and danced like they were performing some kind of cultish ritual for the guy who sat with arms spread wide along the back of a purple velvet couch. Girls writhed around him, for him, leaned in to talk to him. He didn't move for anyone. Asha squeezed. You squeezed back, whispered, "The king." His hair was black, tied in a loose ponytail.

You turn to look at Dylan, move your head slowly, in frames, as if a sudden gesture might cause him and the memory you've just retrieved, to vanish, leaving you a passenger in a driver-less car. His face was thinner then, and his features have since settled into the landscape of his face. Freckles smudge his cheekbones. But his nose, in profile, is still slightly upturned, and his eyebrows still communicate as much as his mouth. It's him, exactly. No one else but him.

"You're so quiet," he says. "What's going on?"

"Gone on," you say. "Past tense."

"Okay, then. What's *gone* on?"

You pass road crews raking steaming asphalt, a gas station hosting a car wash of bikini-clad girls raising money for Alzheimer's research. As the earth beneath your tires turns from pavement to gravel to dirt, the kinked arbutus trees outside your windows appear to bow deeply with an air of ceremony. Eventually you reach the sign where the road forks right toward the trailer: No Thru Road.

THE DRIVEWAY HASN'T been cleared of last winter's windfalls. You and Dylan climb from the car and get to work flinging debris—some of the branches the size of small Christmas trees—into the bushes. You're considering so many things at once. The coincidence of meeting him in this very corner of the forest nearly two decades earlier; the stupidity of driving into the woods—the woods!—with a man you barely know and where your phone has no reception. More than anything you want to text Asha and tell her you're quite possibly living out a modern-day fairy tale. You wonder if the trailer will jog his memory. When he steps inside, he might remember. You pause in your work to look up into the pillared forest. Blue sky. Silence.

Dylan stops, too. "Oh oracle," he says, "what do you see?"

"I'm curious. What do you see?"

"Your hair's green."

"The pipes in my building, they're copper. Stop looking so closely."

You start walking away from him, backwards toward the trailer. You're scared to turn your back. No, not scared. You don't want to miss anything, especially the moment when he recognizes where you've brought him. He regards your awkward retreat with interest. "Careful," he says, when you stumble on uneven ground. Once you've reached the trailer he looks away and resumes clearing the drive.

You consider the morbid vacancy of the place: the rotting blocks on which the structure sags, dirt-streaked vinyl siding, a withered yellow lake toy slung over the doorknob. When *was* the last time Asha came out here? You will have to remind her of its charm, its potential charm anyway. You think you could live out here.

The summer you first spied him in all his adolescent glory isn't so much vivid in your mind as sunk into your bones. You can feel, still, the way they ached at night not only from growing, but also with unformed desires, longings to which you couldn't yet properly attach anything. For the first two nights you and Asha took stock of the way the kids — especially the girls — laughed and moved. After all, your initiation was imminent and you wanted to get it right. Each day you were restless for nightfall. You tossed in the sun and conjured up scenarios where he, the king, invited you to the party, let you sit on either side of him on the velvet couch. You, though perhaps not Asha, were still too innocent to dream up much else.

On the third night, as Asha's father prepared to go into town to pick up his latest girlfriend, you couldn't wait for him to leave.

"I won't be long," he said, "but if those kids come up here for any reason, lock yourselves inside."

"They're just partying," you said.

"What do you know about partying?" Asha's father said.

It was true. This was the first you'd seen of it.

When he finally backed down the drive and his headlights swung up the road, you and Asha hurried into the trees, down to the mossy knoll. There was less activity that night, fewer teenagers and a subdued mood. They sat in the dust around a small fire and looked more childlike than when you'd first seen them dancing and tugging at each other's clothes. Asha squeezed your hand. The couch was unoccupied; the king wasn't in attendance. After waiting all day to see him you felt deflated, rolled onto your back, and looked up into the canopy and beyond to the pricks of starlight. You dug your hands into the moss at your sides until your nails scraped rock. Then a body fell on top of you, across both you and Asha, and clamped his hands over your mouths.

"Don't scream," he said.

His hand on your mouth tasted of rubber and sweat: handlebar grip.

Asha squirmed away and kicked him in the ribs.

"Ow," he said quietly, trying to keep his presence a secret from the others. "Now you have to nurse me back to health."

You rolled away, too, and both of you stood over him for a moment, weighing, you suppose, threat against desire. Wordlessly, the two of you turned and began to walk back toward the trailer, knowing he'd follow.

Inside, his head almost touched the ceiling.

"You're out here alone?" he said.

"My dad will be back soon," Asha said. "It's a summer place."

"Right," he said. "I tried to break in once. He seals it up pretty tight."

You couldn't talk in his presence. You ran your tongue over your teeth and began opening cupboards.

"Anything good in there?" he asked. "I'm starving."

So this picnic isn't the first meal you've prepared in his honour; you've fed him before.

You reheated pasta puttanesca on the hot plate while Asha let him count the jelly bracelets on her wrists. As usual you were wearing matching camisoles and shorts. You still wanted to be identical, but perhaps that night marked a change. When he commented on your twinsy-ness Asha laughed, and you noticed just how short her legs were compared to yours, how she wore a bra beneath her camisole while you so far had no need. You were completely different, so maybe it was time to stop acting like you were the same.

You served him a heaping plate of pasta and you and Asha sat across from him in the trailer's built-in booth while he wolfed it down. For you it wasn't unlike watching Wyatt devour a box of cereal in one sitting, but for Asha, an only child of a broken home, it must have been an early study in the male appetite, its depth and commitment. He didn't once look up from his plate, not until a car came within earshot, chewing up the gravel road toward the trailer, and you and Asha pushed him outside, pointing him down one of the deer trails into the forest. Before he disappeared Asha gave him one of her bracelets which he made a point of stretching over his fist.

"That was weird," she said. "Why'd he want to hang out with us when all his friends are down there?"

But she wasn't really asking a question. She was trying to make real what had suddenly taken on a dreamlike quality;

as soon as he was gone and you were once again standing side by side in the moonlight, in your matching clothes, it was easy to think he'd never been there at all.

YOU DRAG A couple of moldy canvas chairs out from beneath the trailer, fall into one and watch Dylan make a neat stack of the windfall. He seems to have forgotten you, and like Asha all those years ago, you find yourself admiring his single-mindedness. You wonder: can he feel you tracking him through your amber lenses, this man-boy, this near-mythic being from girlhood?

Asha won when she adorned his wrist with her bracelet. Until that moment you hadn't realized it was a competition. The next night he came again to your mossy clearing and this time you knew to walk up the trail and leave them alone. From where you stood you could see, in one direction, the lanterns strung around the trailer and, in the other, the bonfire through the trees. It occurs to you that for most of your adolescence you existed in this in-between state, the lights of others sparking about you while you stood in blackness. It occurs to you that you might still be stuck in this place, and that Asha prefers you there.

"Come," you say. "I want to show you something."

He lopes toward you, wiping his hands on his shorts.

The trail isn't where you remember it. You bushwhack through waist-high salal and alder saplings. Eventually you find the stream bed that signalled your arrival at the mossy knoll, except it has become a swamp thick with skunk cabbage. You sink into mud but plow onward without looking back. What are you planning to show him? A rise in the land, an opening in the trees? Will he recognize it? Will he recognize you?

"Starting to look familiar?" you say.

"Should it?" he asks.

"You said you came out here when you were young."

"I thought I did, but it must have been somewhere else."

"Right here," you say, climbing the rise as though onto the back of a whale. "You and your friends practically set up camp, just over there, where the trees open up. Asha and I spied on you."

He looks at you, bewildered. "No," he says. "I don't think so."

"Think back. In the trailer, you ate pasta, picked out the capers."

He laughs. "I'd never do that."

"You kissed Asha *right here*. This spot was the centre of our universe."

"Your sister-in-law? With the kid?"

You're still wearing sunglasses and when you lift them from your face the trees encircling you and the moss beneath your muddy feet are so varied in texture and colour you don't recognize them as belonging to this world. You feel lightheaded. You think you can feel the earth spinning.

"Are you married?" you ask.

"No," he says.

"Asha saw a ring."

"I took it off."

"So you are. Married."

"Was. She's gone."

"For the weekend? What?" The words come out sounding harsher than you intended, but you're growing impatient. Asha is having babies and you're on an impossible scavenger hunt through your past.

"A bike accident," he says. "Two years ago."

You look to see if he's kidding, but before you can decide your legs fold clumsily beneath you. You claw up a wad of moss and press its spongy coolness against your eyes.

"They say to replace your helmet," you say. "After so many years. Something about the foam. It gets brittle."

"It was more serious than her helmet." You sense him drifting, leaving you.

"I'm sorry," you whisper. "I didn't know."

You feel him settle onto the ground next to you. "I don't like to bring it up. At least not until the second date." The heat coming off him is extravagant. You remove the moss from your eyes and start pulling it apart. "Do you have any idea how long it takes that stuff to grow?" he says, taking the clump and patting it back into place.

No. The heat is coming from you. He presses his palm to your forehead. "You're burning up."

HE DIDN'T COME the fifth night. You and Asha watched him smoking joints and drinking cans of beer on the couch before the bonfire. Did he know you were there? Probably. But he was done with you, a couple of kids. He'd given you your thrill. Now he was looking for his. That night the bonfire had an energy all its own; flames like long ribbons lusted skyward.

"Maybe he'll come later," Asha said, retreating to the tent, then into sleep.

But you stayed awake, waiting for him. And then you heard yelling. Heard them fleeing up the gravel road on bikes. You woke Asha and together you fumbled from the tent and stood for a moment watching the brightness increase through the trees as if by a dimmer switch. It happened that rapidly. Then branches cracking like bones.

"Little fuckers," Asha's father cursed, pulling on his pants and shouting to get in the car. "Should've reported them weeks ago."

There was no phone at the trailer so you had to drive to the nearest house, two kilometres away, to alert the fire hall.

DOES IT MATTER if it was or wasn't Dylan? Whoever he is, he has to carry you out of the forest because your legs will only acknowledge your knees, their remarkable collapsibility. You hear twigs break beneath his shoes, each distinct snap. Also, a car door slamming shut. Wyatt. Asha wasn't kidding. As she wasn't kidding about the ring. She wasn't trying to sabotage you. She doesn't have to. You are your own saboteur.

"Please, put me down," you say. You don't want to emerge from the forest draped across Dylan's arms. What it might look like. What Wyatt might do. Dylan positions one of your arms around his neck and together you limp into the clearing. Wyatt, standing in the trailer doorway, turns at the sound of you approaching.

"Hey," he says cautiously. "Everything all right?"

"Rainey's flu. It just hit me."

Dylan helps you into one of the canvas chairs and gets you some water. "I can take her to a clinic," he says.

"Sure," Wyatt says slowly, doing his brotherly duty: assessing, judging, concluding. "Should have called," he says.

"Sorry," you say. "No reception."

The fire was contained before it reached the trailer but not before sparks rained down on its roof. Once you were permitted, you prowled around the crime scene. Kicked at the purple couch, upholstery burnt away to reveal charred springs. You gained no deeper knowledge of the king and his people because, of course, there was nothing to know except that they'd appeared in your lives at a point when it made sense to pay attention.

"Remember the forest fire out here?" you ask him now. You can't let it go. You want a story out of this, not happenstance.

You want fate, a reason for it all: standing alone in the woods while he and Asha kissed; childless in your mid-thirties; love lost to a bicycle accident.

"Fires out here almost every year," Wyatt says. "Stupid kids."

"Can't blame them," Dylan says. "It's a sweet spot." And as he looks around you think you see a twinge of remembrance cross his face, not just of the fire but also of the girls on the fringe.

"You look familiar," Wyatt says to him. "Play hockey?"

"Don't answer that," you say. "Let's agree that before now we were all strangers."

Ursa Minor

Ursa Minor

HAVING SURVIVED THE HIGHWAY between Port Alberni and Tofino, a two-lane roller coaster frequented by logging trucks, RVs, and locals determined to pass on the gnarliest of curves, Warren pulls into their Green Point campsite with barely enough daylight to pitch their tents. The forecast is rain. After a summer of water restrictions, the outlook for Labour Day weekend is a solid, coastal soaking. When he made the reservation, Warren requested an ocean-view site, but now he sees that the trade-off is exposure; Sitka spruce rise around them like a giant's birthday candles. The lesser canopy, the kind with actual branches from which to string tarps, is nowhere to be found.

Warren climbs from the truck and surveys the teardrop of dirt with its requisite fire pit and picnic table while his brother and tween daughter groan in the cab. Warren had to pull over twice for Troy, not that he deigned to ask Warren directly; both times Troy indicated his need to hurl by slapping the dash, hard and fast. While he never actually vomited, his track record is undeniable; he fouled so many road trips in their youth that Warren didn't want to chance it. Lola, on the other hand, has never been carsick and Warren suspects her groans are only out of sympathy.

"Fresh air," Warren says flatly. "That's what you two need."

Even though daylight is now officially gone, Warren can hear his requested view, the ocean's infinite roar. He walks over to the barricade of knotted salal, the only thing protecting him from a steep slide down to the beach, and looks out to where breakers are winging in from the Pacific. He thinks he can make out their whitecaps; they seem to glow. They *do* glow.

"Hey," he says, calling back to the truck and forgetting his peevishness. "Check this out."

From inside the cab, a sudden thrashing: Troy trying to free himself from the detritus of the five-hour drive. He manages to get around front of the truck, one hand on the hood to steady himself, before releasing a stomach-full of road snacks and coffee in a hot pour around his boots.

"Oh, buddy," Warren says.

Troy whimpers and twists away from his puddle of puke, folding his arms on the hood.

"I'm cold," Lola chatters. She's turned on the light inside the cab and Warren sees she's wearing only a T-shirt, a flimsy thing dusted with sparkles that for months have been decorating his clothes and hair. "Put on your coat," he says, "and help me with the fire."

At the mention of a fire Troy rights himself and lurches toward the pit. "Lola," he says, "come see how it's done." Troy has always fancied himself the better woodsman, arranger of kindling, striker of sparks. Warren is pleased that his brother is not so far gone as to let Warren slop gasoline across a few logs and toss in a match. If only there was a comparable shortcut for erecting the tent. He's heard of a business stocked with all the camping equipment you could possibly need whose employees travel to the site ahead of your arrival to wrestle with tent poles on your behalf. Imagine, he thinks, if all he had to do right now was crack one of his craft ales, impale a few marshmallows for Lola, zip his heartsick brother into a tent, and call it a night. Realistically, that fireside beer might not happen until tomorrow, if at all, depending on the rain's commitment.

Warren climbs into the bed of the truck and begins unloading their gear. He opens Troy's black garbage bag. Inside is a massive down duvet. "That's it? Bro, where's your tent?"

"Gave it to Astrid. I'll sleep in the truck."

"Gave it to her? It's not like you divorced. You broke up."

"We were common-law."

"I liked Astrid," Lola says, putting her hand on Troy's arm.

Warren hops out of the truck. "I heard her say she didn't even like camping."

"It's not your problem how we split stuff up."

"I just hope you didn't screw yourself," Warren says, spreading the groundsheet for his and Lola's tent. As far as he could tell the only things Astrid contributed upon moving in with Troy two years ago were several enormous amateur paintings depicting human forms in various modes of tantric embrace, a bongo drum, and a pair of cat-shredded armchairs. He waits for his brother to say that yes, he at least kept the electronics, but Troy says nothing, only strikes a match and puts it to his perfect teepee of kindling. In the primitive light Warren glimpses his ten-year-old daughter's face. "Are you wearing lipstick?" he says.

"Dad," says Lola.

"What? Are you?"

"It's tinted *chap*stick."

"It looks nice," Troy says, poking at the lengthening flames and emitting one of his trademark sighs, followed immediately by a larger one. Warren can practically count down to his brother's first sob.

"Get over here, you little debutante," he says to Lola. "If you want a castle you can help me build it."

She doesn't protest and comes quickly. To Warren she mouths, *He's crying*. He hands her the tent poles and mouths back, *I know*.

The air is heavy with moisture and already everything feels damp: the sleeping bags Warren pulls from their nylon bags, the groceries and dishes stowed in Tupperware bins. "It is a *rain*forest," he can hear his wife Jana say. Orange light cast by neighbouring fires flickers through the scrubby vegetation on either side of their site, accompanied by the clatter of tin dishware, the tug of a tent zipper. If Jana were here she'd be beautifying their space, spreading the checked tablecloth over the picnic table and setting it with weatherproof lanterns. Instead, his sad sack of a brother is weeping and feeding their fire more and more wood.

"Any bigger and we're going to have a situation," Warren says.

Troy chucks another piece on the flames.

"Fine," Warren says, "you can put it out, too."

He wants to feel bad about the breakup but he can't. Astrid got his back up, right from their first meeting when she called him a HICK — not in the backwoods, without culture sort of way (though perhaps that, too), but HICK as in: house, income, car, kid.

"Income?" Warren said when she dropped the acronym, casually. They were at a lake outside the city. Jana, Lola, and Troy had plunged in as soon as they arrived. Warren was starting in on lunch prep and Astrid, unconvinced of the lake's water quality, stayed to help.

"Yeah, income," she said tersely. "You know, a job you perform in the name of the house, the car, and the kid, but that you don't actually like." They each took corners of a blanket and spread it over a slab of prickly, sun-dried moss. Then Astrid flopped down and began massaging lotion into her tanned legs.

"Hang on," he said. "What if you like your job?" He and Troy were accomplished entrepreneurs. At thirty-eight and thirty-nine years old they owned a contracting company that employed fifty carpenters and sub-tradesmen. Wasn't that everyone's dream, to work for himself?

"Troy tells me you move from one sprawling spec home to the next without stopping to breathe. Why would anyone do that, if not for the money?"

Warren was sweating beneath the blitz of midday sun. He'd forgotten a hat. What had Troy meant, putting it like that? Did he need a break? Want out of the business? Warren pulled the sandwich fixings from the picnic basket and began hacking into an avocado.

"I understand you teach a dance class," he said. Troy had told Warren that Astrid taught modern dance at a community centre once a week. She was otherwise unemployed and, at the age of twenty-nine, still parentally funded.

"It's a process," Astrid said, pulling off her shirt to reveal a bikini top containing fascinatingly small breasts. "Figuring out what to do with your life, what you're passionate about, it takes time."

"Time's a luxury," Warren said automatically. A disorientating sense of déjà vu fell over him like a net. He'd been here before, with other women, some of Troy's past girlfriends. Always petite, always contrary. What was the deal? Was it just a coincidence or did Troy get off on this combination? It's not like he needed a small woman to make him feel big. He was over six feet and had muscles in all the right places. Warren, who was willowy and always struggling to get above a buck sixty, had a theory that Troy had sapped all the nutrients from their mother's womb. Their nicknames as kids had been Major and Minor, as in the constellations Ursa Major and Ursa Minor. Troy was a natural athlete who, at times, had to unplug the family phone to stay the incessant calls from lovestruck girls. Warren did push-ups in his room at night. He ate strategically, to bulk up, but his metabolism was unstoppable. And yet it was Warren who ended up as the brawn in their partnership, showing an unexpected talent for pouring an impeccable concrete foundation, framing a twelve thousand square foot house, determining the precise placement of immense beams. Whereas Troy's talent was in the talk, the charm, the schmoozy securing of clients, ensuring that he and Warren were never without a job.

"Guess Troy was right, you're uncomfortable with alpha-type women." Astrid flipped onto her knees and started rooting through the picnic supplies. "Any chips?"

A burst of adrenaline surged through Warren's body. "He said that?" Christ. How had they, two strangers, gotten here, to the verge of argument?

She shrugged and said, over her shoulder, "Something along those lines."

Warren wanted nothing more than to get away from her, before he said something he'd regret. Troy had misrepresented him. Warren's dislike wasn't gender-specific. It had to do with self-centredness: he didn't like people who dominated a conversation and always found a way to bring it back to her- or *him*self. But he couldn't think of a way to correct Astrid's impression of him without blaming Troy and therefore sounding like the jerk she already thought he was.

Warren looked down to see his hands covered in avocado mush. The paper towels were in the picnic basket. He wiped the guck on his shorts.

Astrid emerged from the basket without the chips, but with Jana's novel. She leaned against a rock and flipped immediately to the back of the book.

"Did you just read the ending?" Warren asked.

"No, the acknowledgements. There's an art to thanking people. If the author gets it right I'll consider reading the book."

"If not?"

"I won't."

How to deal with a person like Astrid, whose judgments were so swift, so final? Warren stood, his filthy shorts a good excuse to go swimming, to get away from her and join the people he loved, the people he thought he understood, who were gathered in the middle of the lake on a submerged rock, standing waist-deep where it should have been impossible. He didn't balk when bits of gravel and rusty fir needles jabbed at the soles of his feet as he made his way to the water's edge. He could have crossed hot coals and not felt a thing.

WARREN AND TROY manage, in the erratic strobe of their head-lamps and the dwindling light of the fire, to string a tarp between the truck's rear bumper and a few fledging cedars that bow deeply under the strain. Then they prop up the tarp's sagging middle with scavenged branches and drag the tent underneath. Throughout the entire graceless process Troy doesn't say a word. They don't need to talk, really, they work that well together, but Troy won't meet Warren's eye. It worries Warren, shunts him back a few decades to when they were kids, when Troy's silent treatment was new and righteous. Grudge was too soft a word. When their parents refused to let him go to a concert in Seattle, unchaperoned at fourteen, he didn't speak to them for a month, exactly thirty-one days. He took all his meals to his room. Weekend nights he came home right on curfew, not a minute before. And even though Warren had nothing to do with their parents' decision—except to loudly point out that if they let Troy go they were setting a precedent that he, Warren, would remind them of when he turned fourteen—he was also ignored for those thirty-one days.

Warren stands back, pretending to take in their lousy handiwork while really observing his brother, trying to unpack the silence, the tortured brow. "If we document this," Warren says, trying to be funny, "no one will hire us again." He holds Troy in the beam of his headlamp.

"The fuck out of my eyes," Troy says, turning away. Warren is relieved. Words, any words at all, are a good sign. He just needs to keep them coming.

The rain starts with sporadic tick-tacks on the tarp as soon as Warren and Lola are tucked in for the night. It seems to Warren that the universe is being kind; it might rain, but it will do so at convenient times, when the campers are most protected and least aware. Lola is already twitching toward sleep, but it will take him longer to get there. Sleeping outside he feels an exciting vulnerability: he spends his days erecting walls to keep the elements out and here he is inviting them in. The sporadic tick-tacking becomes a thundering, pointed assault on their pathetic human shelter. Forget exciting vulnerability, how about plain stupidity? Why, exactly, are he and Troy here? Ah, yes—to let their faces grow stubbly, eat oysters cooked on the fire, and cut off oxygen to the memory of Astrid. Maybe, when Troy is ready, Warren will broach the subject of

Astrid's inadequacies and reassure his brother that by month's end he'll have another girlfriend, with at least two fighting for the role of understudy.

At some point Warren drops into sleep, though not deeply. Part of him remains alert to the punishing rain, and, in the darkest hours, with Lola sleeping corpse-like at his side, he has half-conscious visions of being swept, tent and all, into the eerie surf below.

He wakes feeling broken, as if he *has* gone over the cliff. His Therm-a-Rest has deflated and he's prostrate on the cold, hard earth. He has to pee, badly, but can't move, not yet. The light coming through the orange fabric suggests a day more cheerful than the one he knows exists outside. Still, the rain has eased. Warren sticks his head out the tent flaps and his face is instantly slathered with moisture. In terms of garden hose settings, the spray is set to heavy mist, but with enough layers and Gore-Tex, mist is manageable. Warren pats along the inner seams of the tent. Miraculously, it's dry.

What time is it? Early but not obscenely. Their neighbours have already begun to stir. Warren can hear someone collecting water at the tap across from his campsite. A baby squawks nearby. And underlying it all is the surf, the planet's baseline, which, Warren has discovered, he can choose to hear or not. He wonders how Troy slept in the truck. He didn't once hear a door open or shut. Warren prods Lola's Therm-a-Rest and finds it springy, fully inflated. He contemplates rousing her, making a lesson of the morning set-up, but that would be a breach of camping etiquette. As a kid you're entitled to wait cozy in your sleeping bag until breakfast is ready. It's the adults who have to crawl stiff and dull-headed from their tents and do the work. Warren doesn't begrudge his daughter this luxury, he just wishes

Troy was already out there towelling off the picnic table, mixing pancake batter, and plunging the French press.

Warren hunches out from beneath the tarp, which is sagging in places where rainwater accumulated in the night. He pokes at the small pools, sends them crashing into the mud, then lunges over the bungee chords rigged to the truck's bumper and peers into the cab. There's the passenger seat in deep recline, there's the rumpled duvet, but no Troy. Gone to the washroom? Down to the beach for a contemplative stroll?

Warren pulls the camp stove from beneath the picnic table and hooks up the propane, then carries a battered pot over to the water tap. His surroundings — a thousand different shades of rain-shellacked green — are so vivid that he keeps his eyelids at half-mast as he walks, blurring the scene until it tumbles and beads kaleidoscopically. He's standing awkwardly, trying not to soak himself with the crooked spigot, when he hears Troy laugh.

Warren looks behind him, back into their campsite. He looks up and down the road. Then he hears it again, Troy's affected, confidential laugh, the one he rolls out for prospective clients. Warren takes a few steps down the road with his sloshing pot of water and peers into a neighbouring site. Troy is seated at a tidy picnic table, his back to the road, hands resting on a large glass globe. A young woman sits across from him. When she sees Warren, she raises an arm and waves.

"Bonjour," she says.

"How's it going," Warren says.

Without turning to look at him, Troy says, "Speak of the devil. Meet my lesser brother, Warren."

"He means younger," says Warren, smiling, though Troy's words sting. Ursa Minor. And what does he mean, "speak of the devil"? Have they been talking about him? Has Troy been itemizing Warren's transgressions to this stranger?

"Maude," the woman says, pronouncing it Mode, and rising to shake Warren's hand. "Enchantée." Her grip is intense, the skin of her palm tough, and Warren senses that beneath her Cowichan sweater and loose fleece pants she's sinewy. She wears her hair in two long braids, a style that contradicts her weathered face.

"Café?" Maude asks.

"My saviour," Warren says. He glances around her canopied site — a camper van and two surfboards. "Nice set-up," he says.

"I'm prepared," she says.

"You're committed," Troy says, rolling the glass globe back and forth between his hands.

"Hey," Warren says. "What's with the crystal ball?"

"It floats into my hands when I'm surfing," Maude says. "I thought maybe from a fishing boat, maybe Japan."

"Could be radioactive," Warren says. "Fukushima and all."

Maude hands Warren a mug of blessedly dark coffee, then walks over to a gap in the trees. The coffee roars through Warren's veins and coaxes his heart to a healthy gallop. Screw Troy and his pissy mood, or is he pissy now because Warren's crashed his little party with Maude? It's just as Warren predicted: within twelve hours of their arrival Troy's found a new female friend. He can't help himself; he loves women and they love him back. When they were kids he monopolized their mother, and once he discovered girls he was rarely without one. Now, not only is Troy heartbroken, he's also in his least familiar state: unhitched, a free agent. A serial monogamist on the loose. And who is this Maude, this forest nymph with the Québécois accent?

Warren joins her to survey the swell. At least a dozen surfers are already bobbing beyond the break. He hasn't been surfing in years, wasn't very good at it the few times he tried, but he remembers having fun, floundering in the water, riding the whitewash in to shore.

"It's been a while," Warren says, nodding at the waves. "I could use a refresher."

"A good day for beginners," Maude says. "You can rent gear just up the road."

At least this one seems normal, down-to-earth, not the type to force her agenda on everyone. Not like Astrid, who, the last time he saw her, insisted he and Jana move all the furniture in their living room so she could lead them in modern dance. Lola was an instant disciple, following Astrid's steps precisely, sticking close to her heels, while Jana took heed of the initial instruction and then abandoned it to improvise. Warren was shy at first, hesitant to imitate such large, look-at-me moves, but gradually his self-consciousness fell away. Who was watching, anyway? He was with family. It felt great to lunge about his house without purpose. When he caught sight of his reflection in the French doors he was mesmerized by his stomping feet and windmilling arms, a warrior home from battle recounting his conquests with each thump and thrust. Troy, conversely, shuffled goofily in a corner by himself. He was built for impressive bursts of strength, not nimble like Warren, who made time for yoga most mornings before work. Warren danced with abandon, the three mojitos and his prowess making him feel something like affection toward Astrid, even gratitude. When the song ended and Astrid said, "I need water," Warren said, "Me too," and followed her into the kitchen.

"You're a lunatic out there," she said, her back to him, standing before the sink. "It's like you're possessed."

It could have been a compliment but her tone was like a slap in the face. He saw himself—shirtless, dripping sweat, one of Jana's scarves tied around his head (Lola's touch)—and felt like an idiot. And all for doing what Astrid had encouraged him to do: shed his inhibitions. Maybe she was right, maybe he was possessed. He bodychecked her away from the sink and stuck his head, scarf and all, under the tap.

"Well *excuse* me," she said sarcastically.

Bee stings, that's what he and Troy had called girls' small breasts when they were young and mean; Astrid's were like that. Warren felt her watching him as he let the water run into his ears and eyes. Why didn't she leave? He was on the verge of saying something awful. When at last the cold became too much, he turned off the tap but remained hunched over the sink, dripping. In his periphery he could see Astrid holding out a dish-towel. Forget it. She'd just called him a fool for dancing the way she'd instructed, and now she was offering a truce in the form of a dirty rag? Passive-aggressive. That's what she was. Warren stood upright and shook his head like a dog coming out of water.

"Gross," Astrid said, shielding herself with the rag.

"I thought I was a lunatic?" he said. Why not call her on her immature put-downs?

"Sensitive much?" she said, backing toward the living room.

"More like restrained," he called after her. "Or sure as hell trying to be!"

There was no more dancing after that. When Warren returned from the bedroom in a clean T-shirt, hair combed back, Astrid was yanking her iPod from the stereo. From the couch, Jana was staring at him with narrowed eyes, Lola with round ones, while Troy stood like a bodyguard at the back door, waiting to escort Astrid from the house.

TROY DRIVES INTO town to rent surfboards and wetsuits. It's exactly what they need: exertion, exhaustion, the prospect of brief mastery. The celestial garden hose has shifted settings, from heavy mist to pelting spit, but Warren and Lola are dry beneath their wonky tarp structure. He stands at the camp stove flipping perfectly golden pancakes. She's bundled in her camping chair beside the fire, hunched over one of her dystopic teen novels.

"Stop biting your nails," Warren says.

"I'm at a tense part," Lola says without lifting her eyes from the page, but she balls her fist into her lap. If he recalls correctly, Astrid also bit her nails to the quick. An odd habit, Warren thought, for someone so outwardly confident, and a habit his daughter hadn't developed until recently.

Warren arranges a few pancakes on Lola's plate and douses them with syrup. He takes pleasure in serving her, in setting a large Tupperware lid across her lap like a TV tray. He wishes Jana was here and Troy was not. He'd expected his brother to shake off his funk. To recognize the insignificance of his break-up when standing next to the annihilating force that is the Pacific Ocean, or walking beneath the canopy of five-hundred-year-old trees. But Troy is committed to his bad mood. He is nurturing it.

The irony was that Lola, the disdained *kid* in Astrid's acronym, idolized her. Whenever Astrid and Troy came for dinner, Lola insisted on sitting beside her. Sometimes she would just stand behind Astrid's chair, brushing her hair and adorning it with colourful barrettes. Warren had to admit that even if Astrid didn't want kids of her own, she *was* good with his daughter, listening to her chatter about school and boys, sometimes interjecting with that peculiarly teenage lilt at the end of her sentences. But then she'd go too far. Like the time Warren came home from the barber's to find Astrid perched on the kitchen island, lazily shelling peas while Jana shifted pans inside the oven. Lola was, of course, tucked up beside Astrid, applying temporary tattoos to her shoulders, and didn't look up when Warren came in. Troy was kneeling beside the pantry door adjusting the knob, something Jana had been asking Warren to do for months.

"I was going to get around to that," Warren said.

"Whoa," Astrid said. "Did you enlist or something?"

Jana stopped what she was doing and looked at him. Warren brushed his hand over his head self-consciously.

"You do look kind of severe," she said. "You don't usually go that short."

"Yeah, Dad," Lola said with a conspiratorial smirk at Astrid. "You're practically bald."

"It's just hair," Warren said. "Now stop bothering Astrid and help your mom."

"She's not—" Astrid started, but Warren silenced her with a look.

He knows he's making the same hard face now, remembering that day, the feeling of being an outsider, a joke in his own home. Lola's hand creeps up from her lap and she starts in on her nails again.

"More cakes?" Warren says through clenched teeth. "I guarantee they taste better than your fingers."

"Leave me alone," Lola says with such vehemence that Warren's taken aback. He knows that tone well. It's Astrid, speaking through his daughter.

"You'll get pinworms."

"I don't care."

Warren draws a deep breath, abandons his spatula and frying pan. He walks the perimeter of the site trying to calm himself, trying to shove Astrid from his mind. Through the cedars Warren can see Maude stretching. Familiar poses, tree and eagle. Warren stands out in the rain and clasps his hands behind his back, bends forward with his arms extended above. The opening across his chest sears. He welcomes the pain. Maybe he deserves it. He imagines the two panels of his rib-cage shifting like tectonic plates beneath his skin. Then he unclasps his hands and lets his arms droop to the ground, knuckles brushing the dirt. He is so comfortable in this pos-ition he thinks his fingers could take root. The rain on his neck isn't cold, just a gentle reminder that today he's alive and one day he won't be. Warren empties his lungs in one long breath. Between his legs he sees Troy swing the truck into their site, the bed stacked with fibreglass and fins. His brother's face, viewed upside down and through the windshield, is scowling, tired, handsome. Warren has no idea what to say to him, about anything. Whether it's the stretching, Maude's potent coffee, or the deafening roar of the waves he is soon to be carried aloft on or buried by — his bowels protest. He sets off at a jog for the washrooms before his brother opens the cab door.

WARREN SULKS a little over Troy's board selection: a boogie board for Lola, a short board for himself, and a long board — the kind reserved for novices — for Warren. They squeeze into wetsuits and go to collect Maude. Streamlined in black neo-prene, they all look like smaller versions of themselves: even Troy appears stripped of his bulk; Maude looks positively mini-ature. Walking ahead of Warren and Troy down the trail to the beach, she and Lola resemble a couple of kids. Warren imagines Maude getting tossed around like a puff of sea foam. He elbows Troy and nods at Maude's back.

"So?" Warren says.

"So, what?" Troy says.

Warren thrusts his head at Maude again and says, "You know."

Troy stops walking. "You're unbelievable," he says. "I'm not looking to hook up. We started talking, that's all." Troy snorts and strides ahead of Warren, joining Maude and Lola at the foot of the path where the messy, dripping forest abruptly gives way to beach, sky, water, all of it grey.

Troy and Maude slide on top of their boards and start paddling out toward the break, what Warren recalls as a feat of endurance, the long battle to get out past the onslaught of waves. He and Lola play around in the whitewash. Though they're only waist-deep, the longshore drift sucks them with deceptive speed down the beach. Deceptive because the sixteen identical kilometres of sand make it impossible to distinguish where they started from where they're headed. Warren catches occasional glimpses of Troy and Maude resting atop their boards now that they've made it beyond the break. Moments later Troy pops up, rides the wave a few metres, then bails. His board shoots up like a bath toy in the roiling surf and Warren knows his brother is getting pounded under the waves. He realizes he's holding his breath, as Troy must be, and releases it. A few seconds later, Troy surfaces, groping about for his board. Maude catches the next wave and Warren admires her friskiness as she carves expertly and pumps to gain more speed. She makes it look easy. Warren wants to get out there and give it a try.

"Hey Dad, I'm a sea otter," Lola says. She's given up the boogie board after taking a few lungfuls of salt water and is now wallowing in a large tidal pool, collecting shells along her chest.

Warren flops down beside her. He likes wearing a wetsuit, his body warm when otherwise he'd be hypothermic.

"What do you say I go out there for a bit? I'll ask Troy to come in. You won't be alone long." Lola chews her index finger, deliberating. Warren holds his tongue.

"Can I pee in my wetsuit?" she says finally. "People do, right?"

"All the time."

Paddling out to meet Troy and Maude, Warren ignores the twinge of guilt at leaving Lola unattended on the beach. But what harm can possibly come to her on that sandy expanse? He fights through the waves, turtle rolls under incoming swells and feels their energy surge overhead, trying to rip the board from his hands. That's all it is, all *he* is: energy, sometimes misguided and other times, like now, startlingly precise. He rolls out of a wave and on top of his board. Water spills from his ears.

"Real smart," he hears Troy say. "You left Lola alone?"

Warren sits up, astride his board. "She's fine," he says. "Besides, I thought you could hang out with her for a bit." Warren looks to where his speck of a child is now up on her feet, probably searching for shells, or a different pool to pee in. Having just ridden a wave almost to shore, Maude is ferrying herself back out to Warren and Troy with preternatural speed.

Troy shakes his head. "Mushy out here anyway."

Warren yanks a strip of kelp from around his ankle and tosses it lamely in his brother's direction.

"Having fun?" Maude calls when she's within earshot. Her face is pink from the salt and exertion. Her braids are wound up around her head, lumpy beneath her hood. Still, Warren thinks she looks great. "I was watching you," he calls. "You're really good." Troy's head whips around and for a fleeting moment he focuses twin beams of hatred on Warren. What? Should Warren not compliment her? Should he not talk to her at all?

"Go ahead," Warren shouts. "Get it out of your system." He paddles to stay abreast with Troy. It feels ridiculous confronting his brother in this position, on his stomach, and in this environment, where they're supposed to be tuning in to the ocean's cosmic pulse.

"You just met her," Troy says, flicking water in Maude's direction, "and you're nicer to her than you were to Astrid."

"Nicer? All I did was try to be nice."

"Exactly, *try*, and not very hard. You're a jerk to all my girlfriends. If I started seeing Maude, you'd be a jerk to her too." Maude glances at Warren but paddles away. Who knows what Troy's told her.

"Not true," Warren says.

"No one's good enough for you. Only Jana and Lola. No one else is allowed in. You made Astrid uncomfortable every time she came around."

"I made *her* uncomfortable?" Warren wishes he could stop the water moving beneath him. He wishes for something solid to brace himself against. "How about choosing someone who's nice to me for a change?"

"You?" Troy lets out a fearsome yell. "She was nice to *me*. Why isn't that enough?"

Warren awkwardly turns his massive hunk of foam inland. Screw this. All he's been is supportive. The whole drive up here, putting up with Troy's silence. Trying to see it as a symptom of heartache, and be sympathetic.

Just then Maude, who's been sitting cross-legged on her board about twenty metres off, calls out: "Here comes a set. Something for everyone."

Warren's stomach actually quivers. He can't believe how small he feels, and how arrogant, drifting blithely on the planet's most destructive force. Maude is the only one quick enough to position herself in time for the first wave. It hasn't quite reached them, but even in the distance Warren can sense it building, how big it's going to be. He turns to check on Lola. She's waded back into the waves. Warren flings his arms overhead in a gesture he hopes conveys alarm to his daughter: *go back, get out.*

Many things happen then but to say they happen all at once would be wrong. Warren notices, too late, that he's caught inside the wave, facing inland; it's about to break on top of him, maybe break him in half. Water cascades down the face of the wave while its crest continues to rise. Just before it thrusts him under, Maude zips past: crouched, loose, face of calm. Does she acknowledge Warren, his dire position? No time to say. The wave slams down on top of him and he is being waterboarded, the entire Pacific Ocean plunged through his nose. The pressure flattens him, splays him so that any solid object coming from above or below—a rock, his surfboard, a piece of driftwood—might kill him, impale his soft core. The wave powers shoreward, dragging and tumbling him across the sandy bottom. When at last the pressure eases, he begins to rise. On the surface his mouth instinctively forms an O, a vacuum to draw in the maximum amount of air. Everything burns. Eyes, throat, lungs. It's a miracle his surfboard is still leashed to his ankle. He clings to it, flaps around trying to lock onto Lola, but he's surfaced into a trough and another wave is bearing down. Have mercy, he thinks. But before it can hammer him Troy moves in, grim-faced, murderous. He flips Warren on his board with the same ease as he tossed him when they were teenagers wrestling in the backyard. So this is how it ends. But this wave builds more slowly than the last, it slams down with less brutal force. He is better positioned to take it. Troy saw what was coming and positioned him.

Warren rolls out of the wave gasping. He flounders atop his board and manages to slide under the next wave just in time. He pushes himself up and searches for Lola, strains to locate her on shore. Please let her be safe, not caught in a rip tide, not headed for Japan. He looks to where he thinks he last saw her but how far has he been pulled down shore? Maybe he's way off the mark. Then he sees Troy emerging from the surf, heading toward a tidal pool where Lola's leaning back on her elbows, slapping her feet against the water like flippers.

"A little big for you, this wave?" Maude says. Where has she come from? Warren can barely move; his arms and legs hang off his body like tubes of wasted flesh. His tongue, too, is a sea slug in his mouth. He grunts, yes.

"You need to know how to handle yourself. People die out here every year."

Good god, is she really lecturing him? Is she really getting into downward dog on top of her board? Salt water continues to pour from his nostrils, his mouth, his eyes. Troy is collapsed beside Lola now, the two of them watching him, awaiting his next move. Troy tosses Warren the finger. Astrid wasn't right for his brother, Troy would have figured that out eventually. But in the meantime, Warren shouldn't have pushed her away. He should have let Troy talk about her. Listened to him uncritically. He should have allowed Astrid's ghost to leap and spin around the campsite until she faded off into the trees. Warren stretches out on his board, head down in supplication. He closes his eyes and slips his arms into the liquid muscle that almost killed him, that without help from anyone propels him toward shore.

Firestorm

Firestorm

"**CHERRIES**," says Rachel. "Pull over."

"What?" says Rory. "Where?"

"Now!" she says. "There!"

Rory veers too sharply onto the shoulder, spitting gravel.

"There was a sign," says Rachel. "And arrows."

"I believe you."

"It's not a question of what you *believe*. The arrows were red."

The fruit stand is a moth-coloured barn backed by orchards, backed by mountains. Flats of cherries are arranged in a pyramid in the shade. A girl on a stepladder retrieves the crowning box at each customer's request. Then she adjusts the pyramid, sets another flat on top.

"Too young for you," Rachel says. She tosses her flip-flops from the car and steps down into them.

"Not if I'm the pervert you're suggesting I am." Rory climbs out, then heads for the shade of the barn. "In that case, she's just fine."

RACHEL AND RORY, Rory and Rachel: high school sweethearts, a classification that makes them both gag.

"It just worked out that way," Rachel says to the people who treat them like a freak show, who ask in voices that betray a mixture of envy and horror, how she and Rory made it work, how they didn't blow apart during those experimental years when they were supposed to be treating their brains to chemicals and "finding themselves" via random sexual encounters on Thai beaches. "It's not like we planned it," Rory says. "It's not like we thought it would last." But it did, they did, like an astronaut's footsteps forever recorded on the bland surface of the moon. And yet, let's be honest, privately they are smug. By the time they're twenty-seven they've been together ten years. When friends celebrate two years of fidelity they offer *good for you*, and later speculate on how long until one of them flails. A relationship might begin with attraction, fleshy and whole-hearted, but beyond that it's discipline. Rachel and Rory, then, an unflappable regiment, a two-person platoon, each serving as medic, lieutenant, and spiritual counsel to the other. Nothing gets between them, nothing and no one. Until, of course, someone does.

"I might sleep with someone," is Rachel's latest threat from behind her barricade of pillows. "Just to be fair."

And while fairness is one of her gripes, it's not the main one. Rory has sullied their track record, rendered them ordinary. Now they belong to the same stock as their hither and thither friends. Now they're just part of the monoculture: unexceptional, prone to blight.

KEREMEOS, in the Okanagan valley, has always been Rory's favourite pit stop when driving inland, away from Vancouver, and crawling out from beneath the rain shadow of the Coast Mountains. Gnarled orchards line the single road through town, pumping out fruits of spectacular sweetness. Rory draws the desert climate, an unfamiliar dryness, into his fog-soaked lungs, but today there's no pleasure in it. Rachel has ruined it for him by sulking through the traffic-clogged Fraser Valley and by eschewing all music in favour of news updates on the forest fires burning around Kelowna, which happens to be on their planned route. And now with the accusation.

Rachel's sifting through the flat of cherries on her lap, tossing the overripe ones out the window. Rory would like to eat those, but in the name of silence and momentary peace he lets them go. A news bulletin solemnly details evacuations and road closures. A resident of the area describes sparks gusting like intergalactic rain. They are still one hundred kilometres away from the fires but already Rory smells smoke.

Beneath their tires the road is a ribbon of blank tape. They are driving to a wedding in the Rocky Mountains, to the cusp of a glacial lake where Rachel's childhood friend Charlotte will marry Evan, an anaesthesiologist with a high, round ass — Ass Man, Rory calls him. Rory's permitted to mock Evan, but never Charlotte. Charlotte, with whom Rachel hasn't spent any real time since her early teens, is off limits. Rory didn't even meet her until he and Rachel hosted a housewarming party in their first apartment, a year out of high school. They provided a keg but Charlotte, who happened to be home from McGill visiting her parents, brought champagne. She was the only one who contributed anything and might as well have been the only guest the way she monopolized Rachel, the two of them polishing off the bubbly in the bedroom. When they did emerge to circulate, briefly, Rory thought Charlotte resembled a giraffe. "You can only go up from here," she said, taking in the walls he and Rachel had lovingly painted calypso orange. As she spoke, her neck seemed to extend toward him while she held the rest of her body at a slight remove, giving the impression she might

swivel away at any second. Rory shared his zoological observation, the kind Rachel typically appreciated, once the keg was
empty and their friends had left. She was drunk, sure, but it
actually scared him the way she went from sleepily gathering
plastic cups to intense rage.

"Apologize," she demanded.

"What?"

"I'm Charlotte. Tell me you're sorry."

"That's stupid."

"Think before you speak."

"I shouldn't have to, not with you."

Rachel chucked the stack of cups at him. Dregs of beer soaked
his shirt and the glossy parquet floor they'd been so enamored
with upon moving in.

"Silverfish," Rory said. "Miss Perfect made a point of telling
me she spotted one tonight."

"Oh, god," Rachel moaned and sank to the floor.

"What's the big deal?" Rory said. "They're only in the bathroom."

"I've seen them in the cupboards."

"She's a snob," he said. He was wasted, too, but felt focused,
crystalline. He shoved his hands into Rachel's armpits and
hauled her up. She refused to take the weight so he flung her
onto the couch and then, panting, leaned out the window and
shouted, "I'm sorry, queen Charlotte. I'm so fucking sorry."

"Shut up," Rachel whispered. "Just go to bed."

But he hadn't. In his drunken clarity he'd washed the dishes,
mopped the floors, and spray-cleaned all surfaces of any evi-
dence of celebration. What had they been talking about in the
bedroom anyway, Rory wanted to know when at last he flipped
the deadbolt on their apartment door? If Rachel had still been
awake he'd have asked, but the next morning when she brought

him coffee in bed it seemed pointless to revisit the previous night. And over the years, whenever Charlotte visited, always ignoring Rory and locking Rachel away in some room that would then leak the goopy sounds of girl bonding, he convinced himself he didn't care. What did begin to concern him, though, was the after-effect of their get-togethers; each time Rachel was released back to him she was curt and sullen. Dissatisfied, he could only assume. When she studied the trajectory of her life next to Charlotte's it depressed her. Rory began to suspect they were talking about him, his inability to make Rachel happy, and over the years his dislike for Charlotte metastasized.

"Will you please slow down?" Rachel says. "Why are you riding that guy?"

Rory hadn't realized. "Sorry," he says, easing off the gas. "Thinking about stuff."

"Our funerals?"

"The wedding. Ass Man." If Rachel smirks he misses it.

"He buys her antique lingerie."

"Antique? As in, previously worn?"

Rachel shakes her head and looks out the passenger window.

"Do *you* want antique lingerie?"

"I didn't say drive like my grandmother."

Traffic in the oncoming lane clears and the impatient line of cars behind them slaloms past and disappears down the highway through the ribs of rising heat. On either side, brown mountains appear to be crumbling. Chalky boulders line the road.

"It's like the doldrums," Rachel says. She dangles two cherries, connected like a wishbone, over Rory's ear. The brush of her fingers against his skin sparks a vibration in his jawbone. When they were younger they discovered that sometimes, when their foreheads touched, what felt like a current of electricity would run between their skulls. It tickled and when they pulled their heads apart the skin itched. Rory clacks his teeth to stop the vibration, but it persists. In the near distance a couple of hitchhikers sit hopelessly on backpacks at the side of the road.

"Sorry, dudes," Rory says as they fly past. But Rachel is craning in her seat.

"Turn around," she says.

"Rach, their sign says Kelowna. We're not going that far today." Rory keeps driving, one hand on the wheel, the other massaging electricity from his jaw.

"Turn around."

"Since when do we pick up hitchhikers?"

"I said turn the goddamn car around." She's looking at him with eyes like jailbirds winging free.

This time he can't ignore her.

"HEY," Rachel says, carefully arching her upper body out the open window to avoid touching the hot metal frame. "You guys need a lift?"

"Are you kidding?" says the one with a pierced eyebrow. "You're a goddess. Some kids in the back of a station wagon just flipped us the finger."

They're younger than Rachel and Rory, though not by much. She likes the way they've wrapped т-shirts around their heads like Bedouin head scarves.

"Trunk's full," Rory says, swiping at the cherries hooked over his ear. "You'll have to put your bags on your laps."

Before climbing in, the hitchhikers unravel their turbans and pull the т-shirts over their torsos. Shame, Rachel thinks, cryin' shame.

"Noah," says the pierced guy as he folds his long limbs behind Rory's seat, then points to his stocky companion, "and that's Chad." Rachel releases her ponytail and fluffs her hair across her shoulders. She knows Rory's watching but doesn't care. With strangers in the back seat she's forced out of her head. She's forced to entertain. It's a relief. Doesn't Rory know punishing him is a grim job? It wears on the psyche. Thanks to his sorry behaviour they are effectively marooned on inhospitable terrain. She's a klutzy hiker even on cedar-chip paths, but out here she's clueless, bushwhacking, smacking rocks together in hopes of creating fire, the kind that will raze whole mountains to the ground.

"What's in Kelowna?" Rachel asks, turning in her seat to get a better look at their passengers.

"Party," says Noah.

"A fucking good time," says Chad.

"A good time," Rachel says, looking at Rory's tight profile, his eyes squinting behind sunglasses as if he'd like to shut them completely and be done with it, with her, right here, right now. "I could be into that."

RORY UNDERSTANDS THAT as the betrayed party Rachel has the right to lay it on thick, to subject him to something of a re-initiation. And if he can take it, moreover if he takes it without protest, they can begin again. He also understands it's on him to court her for a second time. Clean the ring from the tub, bring home takeout mid-week, learn, finally, to hang his coat by the door. But this, what's she thinking? Is he supposed to keep quiet while she practically propositions strangers? For the first time in years Rory doesn't know what she's up to and it terrifies him. He looks over at her in the passenger seat— serene-faced, sunblocked, the very picture of Oil of Olay—and panic shanks him between the ribs.

"We're not actually going as far as Kelowna," Rory says, glancing in the rear-view. "We'll drop you at the next junction. Maybe you'll have better luck there."

"We're going to a wedding," Rachel explains. "But we've given ourselves a few extra days."

"We have plans tonight," Rory says.

"We do?" Rachel says. "Can we cancel them?"

"No."

She harrumphs back into her seat.

"We're already late," says Chad. "Party's going off."

Mountains flatten into hills and soon they're cruising with the beach traffic along Skaha Lake. The air is gauzy with smoke, but vacationers persist; bathing-suited families throng the causeway hauling inflatable water toys and coolers. Beyond the beach, arid bluffs are interrupted by irrigated bursts of green.

"Vineyards," Rory says. Their plans—a surprise—involve a night in a Tuscan-inspired villa on the grounds of a winery. Rory booked it after reading positive online reviews. The restaurant is apparently a feat of glass and light, a pod that, once inside, gives diners the impression they're hovering above the lake. Isn't that what they need, a little levity? And isn't this the sort of thing he's supposed to do to win her back? Rory glances sideways at Rachel to see if she's picked up on his clue, but she only gulps indifferently from her water bottle.

At a crosswalk they wait for the colourful hordes to pass. Rachel sticks her arm out the window and pianos her fingers on the roof, rings clattering like hail.

"Hey," she says, flipping around in her seat, "you guys feel like a swim?"

"Hell, yeah," says Noah.

"Nah," says Chad, "we can't waste any more time."

"You're disgusting," says Noah, "and you smell."

"Find somewhere nice," Rachel instructs Rory. "Away from the riff-raff." She flicks her hand at the general populace on the main beach, then reaches beneath her shirt, unclips her bra, and whips it off. She pulls her bikini top from the bag in her footwell and strings herself into it as only a woman can, skillfully, without showing everything, though still showing too much for Rory's taste. But then, he's no longer entitled to taste.

"Do you know where you're going?" Rachel asks when he turns onto a dirt road riddled with cattle guards.

"We're parallel with the lake. The road will spit us out sooner or later."

"You don't, then," she says, sitting tall in her seat, her vertebrae releasing a series of snaps. "Just say you don't know."

The road ends in a dusty parking lot. Theirs is the lone car. Noah and Chad could easily roll them, jack the car, and be on their way to Kelowna. Rory takes his time pulling the parking brake and waits for the others to climb out before cutting the engine. Truth is, he doesn't have a bad feeling about these guys, at least not the menacing kind. They're just dudes trying to get to a party, an enviable goal. Rory wipes the sweat from his face and chokes down a handful of trail mix to quash the nausea he feels at the picture framed in the windshield: Rachel slathering Noah with sunscreen, her fingers tracing a tattoo across his back, script so ridiculously elaborate Rory can't make out what it says.

"Come on, bro," Chad says, gesturing impatiently to Rory.

Rachel snaps the lotion shut. Clearly Rory won't be receiving a rubdown.

They take the only path off the parking lot into seemingly

infinite grassland. Rory stops at the trailhead to read a legend displaying wildlife they might encounter: bighorn sheep, Western screech owl, rattlesnakes. Up ahead, Rachel's laughter sounds like the call of an animal. Rory puts his head down and follows at a distance he hopes conveys both his irritation over the detour as well as his acquiescence.

The path twists and climbs along the east shore, for a time following a ridge above a campground; the smell of barbecued meats mingles with combusting swaths of Douglas fir and ponderosa pine dying acrid deaths just north of them. Rory continues to hang back, waiting to see if Rachel will turn and check that he hasn't slid to his death or fallen into a snake pit, but only Chad glances over his shoulder. When Rory finally decides to close the gap, too curious about the conversation he's missing, he overhears Rachel saying, "All this white rock and turquoise water. It makes me think of Greece."

"Azure," Noah says, then says it again.

He has a rock-climber's physique. Rory's flailed around in climbing gyms enough times to know. He's watched guys like Noah, tall and lean with inflated-looking shoulders, ascend with ease. Classically handsome, Rory thinks. But is there anything *unique* about him, other than the eyebrow thing and the tattoo which Rory's had plenty of time to discover reads *Primate*? Rachel used to tell Rory she liked his caveman appearance, his prominent occipital ridge and gimped ribcage, the misaligned right panel jutting beneath his flesh as if slightly ajar. His treasure chest, she said. Rory imagines having *Neanderthal* tattooed across his own back. Would that make him attractive to her again?

Rachel steps from the path and starts skidding down the loose cliffside. "I'm dying to get in that water," she says. "It's suffocating out here."

From a rocky outcrop they take turns diving into the lake. Balmy wind carrying ash from the fires creates choppy swells across the surface. Rachel swims in large circles sighing to no one in particular: "What could be more beautiful than this?" Rory couldn't disagree more. He feels deadened and dismal. Noah puts his face in the water and threads a precise stroke toward the middle of the lake. Chad rubs his scalp and face, dutifully cleansing himself, then climbs out and rolls a joint. Rachel and Rory are left alone for a moment, treading water.

"Having fun?" Rory asks.

"Tons." Rachel says. "You?"

"You have no idea."

Not far off a speedboat carves the lake's surface. A waxy white fang.

"My disappointment is hard to measure," Rachel says. "Every day I hate you, even if it's only for a few seconds."

"Why are we going to this wedding?"

"I'm telling you how I feel."

They fall silent when they hear Noah's stroke returning. Rory slips underwater and makes for the rock. Rachel might leave him. He hadn't thought it would go this way or this far. She'd wanted to have sex with him immediately after he'd told her of his screw-up, which, by then, was a few months past. He'd thought that meant she'd forgiven him, that there was stuff to work out, sure, but basically she was telling him it would be okay. He hoists himself from the water and strains to hear what Rachel and Noah are saying a little ways offshore. But the wind is too high and the distance too great to make out anything more than the tones of two people getting along.

RORY AND CHAD are stoned. Rachel shepherds them into the back so she can converse with a straight person while she drives. Once she gets up to speed on the highway she asks Noah to spread a towel across her backrest so her hair doesn't drench the upholstery. She leans forward, barely, and allows herself the pleasure of his arm brushing against her skin. A sign for the winery — Rory's surprise — streaks past. She'd seen a printout of the reservation on their desk at home, not tucked away or even turned over. Kelowna isn't too far out of their way. She'll drop these guys then head back so she and Rory can resume whatever it is they're in the process of doing. Maybe she'll call Charlotte tonight and tell her what she knows. Abandon her plans of a big reveal while the two of them sip champagne in Charlotte's bridal chambers as the guests arrive. Why not drop her bomb over the phone and let Charlotte dread their arrival, the commotion Rachel will promise to cause, the tale she'll tell to anyone who will listen. Because for some reason it's Charlotte she's most furious with. Rory was stupid and weak, yes, but Charlotte was cruel, and has been since Rachel first knew her in middle school.

Has Rachel forgotten about being made to walk several feet behind Charlotte's clique as they wound their way through the neighbourhood after school? Does one ever forget that first bitter experience of rejection? No, one does not. Charlotte claimed Rachel's laugh was obnoxious, so grating she couldn't think straight. Her laugh? How had it suddenly become annoying enough to have her expelled? But Rachel wasn't the only one. The shunning rotated with regularity. Charlotte was always scheming: favouring one girl just when it looked as though she might defect, pushing another out on the flimsiest of pretexts. When she travelled with her family to Hawaii one winter, she gave Rachel and a few other girls quarters. Every day at noon, before opening their lunch bags, they were to close the coins in their left hands and think of Charlotte bodysurfing in her pink bikini. Rachel was given the task of keeping a log and reporting on which friends failed to observe the ritual. The tyranny might have ended when Charlotte transferred to a private high school, but she'd managed to keep her hooks in Rachel, getting her to report back on their friends, who had a crush on whom, who had spoken badly of Charlotte since she left, who was getting fat. Even when they grew older, graduated, and Charlotte attended first McGill, then law school, she enlisted Rachel's assistance in editing essays and applications. Charlotte gave her deadlines and Rachel, barista by day and waitress by night, never missed one.

Like Rory, then, Rachel was also stupid and weak, and she didn't change in the intervening years. She didn't protect herself, or Rory. Still, she can't help being so terribly disappointed in him. He's let down their squadron, lit a fire in the trench. Though his big confession didn't initially include with whom, it was obvious. If Rachel thought about it, thought back, Rory went from avoiding any mention of Charlotte's name to using it freely in conversation. How could he think Rachel wouldn't know?

"Feed me a cherry," Rachel says, and nods to the flat jammed over the parking brake. Noah presses one firmly inside her mouth, his thumb remaining on her lips a second longer than necessary. Bold, she thinks, and turns to spit the stone out her window. She glances in the rear-view to see Rory kneading his jaw as if he's been punched.

"Another, please." And then Noah keeps them coming, one for her, one for him, his fingertips growing dark with the juice.

WHEN CHAD OFFERED Rory a toke back at the lake he felt he had to accept (not to would have made him appear even more up-tight), but almost as soon as the smoke touched his lungs he knew it was a mistake. As he looked out at the glorious picture of summer before him—the lake's vivid water, Rachel star-fished on her back—melancholy ballooned inside him, made him groan aloud.

"You okay, man?" Chad asked.

"Strong," Rory said, coughing.

"Your sister's flirting pretty hard. She *is* your sister, right?"

Rory laughed. Rachel his petulant little sister. So that's how it looked, how they came across. He didn't actually think it was funny—just as he isn't amused by the game of cherries going on in the front seat—but he didn't correct Chad.

When Rory rolls down his window the breeze offers no re-lief. The smoke outside is sharp, close. Up ahead he can see cars slowing, brake lights piling up. Rachel slows too, then stops. He looks at her bare shoulders and follows the length of her arms to her hands, loose on the steering wheel. He knows how her skin would feel against his, cool from swimming but quick to warm.

"What's going on?" Rachel says.

Noah, shirtless again, sticks his head out the passenger win-dow. "Cars aren't even idling. Everyone's just stopped."

"Primate," Rory says.

"What?" says Rachel.

"Your tattoo," says Rory.

"Yeah?" says Noah.

"Sort of stating the obvious."

"Sure, maybe. Or a reminder of our animal nature."

"You need a reminder?"

Rory opens his door and climbs out, stumbles over the concrete barrier separating the highway from a thin strip of shore. A water bomber careens into view, fills its tank, and then disappears over the treeline, which is aglow, though not with sunset. A radio announcer blaring from inside someone's car reports that flames are leaping across lanes, the highway is closed indefinitely. Chad joins him and starts chucking rocks into the lake.

"Maybe the planets are trying to tell me something," he says.

Rory sits, puts his head between his knees. "Someone expecting you at that party?" he asks. He has no trouble recalling that feeling of expectancy, excitement. It was like that for him, too, once. Only now it's dread that churns inside him when he reaches their apartment door. Will Rachel be there? How will she look at him? What will she say? Chad doesn't respond so Rory looks up and finds him frozen in mid-throw. To their left a deer has materialized. She wades into the water to drink. On her flanks, where there should be fur, Rory sees flesh and the rawness of it. She must have come through the fire. She drinks and drinks, keeping a dark marbled eye on them. She wades deeper, until water sloshes beneath her belly. Then she starts to swim.

THE BLUE STREAM MOTEL, about a kilometre before the highway closure, has one room left.

"We might as well take it," Rachel says, still not acknowledging their reservation at the vineyard, or that it might be time to lose their companions. She prefers to make Rory fume, which he does, quite visibly, stalking grim-faced into the lobby and returning with a key to room 308. Rachel imagines doing an impression of him: sweaty, stoned man not getting his way. Sweaty, stoned man in a fix. Sweaty, stoned man did this to himself.

"Get out," he says to Rachel, still in the driver's seat.

"Relax," she says. "We're all getting out."

"Not him," Rory says, pointing at Chad. "We're going for beer."

"We'll all go. It's no big deal," Rachel says.

"No," Rory says, opening her door.

Rachel isn't sure how it happens but somehow she and Rory trade places and then he's shoving the box of cherries at her through the window.

"What the fuck?" she hisses.

"You wanted fair, so here's your chance."

"A stream, come look," Noah calls to her. He's standing on a small footbridge painted royal blue, the same colour as the doors to the motel rooms in the building beyond. He seems perfectly harmless but how can she know for sure? Flirting with Noah had been safe when Rory was within reach, tracking her in the rear-view mirror. But she'd pushed him too far. She watches the car turn around and disappear onto the highway. How could he put her in this position?

"There are actual fish in here," Noah says.

"Yeah?" she hears herself say, because Rory's right, she wants to, wants a reason to go to Noah, wants to make a choice the way Rory did, completely on her own. "What kind of fish?" she says. But Noah's already climbing the stairs toward the third floor. His footfalls up each concrete flight are light and eager. Rachel follows but doesn't hurry. She tries not to think about Rory, only of herself.

Noah unlocks the door. "Seventies chic," he says and disappears inside.

She pauses on the landing and looks across the highway to the lake, the humps and shoulders of parkland on the far side blazing, a true firestorm. If Rory were here they'd stand side by side, each silently taking in the destruction. Being with Rory has always been like being alone. Only better. With Rory there was no chase, no need for a lasso. He just appeared halfway through her graduating year, eclipsing World Wars and Shakespeare. He made the decline of the Roman Empire seem like old news.

Inside, she finds Noah fallen back on the bed, limbs flung wide.

"Smoke's harsh," he says. "Shut the door."

THE DRIVEWAY IS long and smooth, winding up through the vineyards toward the villas and restaurant.

"What are we doing?" Chad asks.

"Quick stop," Rory says, shutting off the music and hoping Chad doesn't say anything else, just lets him be for a moment, imagining Rachel beside him taking in the surprise. But as hard as he tries, all he can picture is Charlotte, in town for Christmas and needing a ride in from the airport. Rachel was at work so Rory had gone grudgingly in rush-hour traffic, all the while dreading the drive back into town, their usual awkward silence stretching, even under good conditions, to at least thirty minutes of pure discomfort. But this time she was different. He could tell even as he approached the terminal and saw her standing at the curb, luggage and a bag of wrapped presents at her feet, coat pulled close. It was the way she was looking out for him, anxious, as if she was worried he might not show.

"Thanks for coming," she said. There was an apology in her voice, and Rory interpreted it as one that encompassed all the years she'd ignored him.

"No problem." The bitterness he'd cultivated on the drive out evaporated like jet fuel into the cold night. They took a meandering route in from the airport to avoid traffic and talk was easy, an actual conversation. It was embarrassing how badly he wanted to be seen by Charlotte. At one intersection they passed a pub made to look like a Tudor manor and Charlotte suggested they stop for a pint, a little Christmas cheer. Sure, why not? He parked away from the other cars in the lot though he couldn't say why. Charlotte might even have directed him to the spot, her hand on the wheel. "A master manipulator," Rachel said when he finally couldn't keep it to himself any longer. She didn't even seem surprised. "You don't see it happening, and the next thing you know she's given you her passwords and you're up past midnight filling out applications for her online." So that was the reason for the furrowed brow, the sullen demeanour after Charlotte's closed-door visits. Rachel couldn't say no. And apparently neither could Rory. Charlotte was crashing into him before he'd put the car in park.

RACHEL AND RORY, Rory and Rachel: lucky and in love before twenty. He is her measure for every man. In the motel bathroom she cups handfuls of water to her mouth. Her lips sting, the insides of her cheeks are raw, and her stomach feels queasy from all the cherries. In the other room Noah has flicked on the news.

"Come see these aerial shots," he says.

Lightning strikes have caused the fires. High winds are wreaking havoc. She and Rory might not make it to the wedding at all. Standing before the smeary bathroom mirror, Rachel revises her plan. She will save her confrontation for a more intimate dinner with the newlyweds, perhaps once the honeymoon is over and all the thank-you cards have been sent. Poor Evan, learning too late the dirty truth about the woman he married. And poor Rory having to sit through all of it. But it's the least he can do, and he's agreed to do whatever it takes. She mustn't forget to tell him about the mule deer that stepped out of the roadside ditch and passed right in front of their car. Rachel watched the animal hop the concrete barrier and move down to the water's edge. After bending her head to drink she started swimming. Where was she going? Was she lost, confused? What about instinct? There were no islands that Rachel could see, no boggy mounds where the deer might find respite, just the other side, in flames.

What Are You Good At, What Do You Like to Do?

What Are You Good At, What Do You Like to Do?

IT WAS LATE on the first day of winter. I was walking home from a staff Christmas party where I'd danced too close with an employee and was feeling at once jubilant and stupid about our swaying in what I thought was a discreet corner of the Greek restaurant rented for the occasion. I was going home to no one, but he was going home to a girlfriend and I wondered how he was feeling about our encounter, if I'd awakened some dormant passion or if he just felt pent up, due to the close dancing, and maybe a bit guilty, too.

I had politely refused the prepaid taxi ride home, offered to me by the boss. "It's a beautiful night," I said, "and I don't have far to go, but thank you." She'd accompanied me outside, presumably to make sure I was okay to walk, maybe even for a little informal vetting.

"You don't know a single person here, do you?" she said, crossing her arms against the cold. "I mean, you're no one's guest. You're not even a former employee."

"No," I said. "And actually I live quite far."

"You're nuts," she said. "What did you do, just walk in off the street?"

I admitted that yes, I had. I'd been walking past the restaurant's picture window and seen an elegant crowd mingling inside, everyone gussied up in holiday finery, so I went in and sat at the bar. No one told me it was a private party and the bartender didn't appear to have a problem with my being there. I ordered a glass of wine and waited for the handsome Italian-looking man devouring canapés at the other end of the bar to notice me.

"Wow, you're unbelievable," the boss said. "I mean, who does that?"

"Take it as a compliment. I don't go to many of these things. All those Secret Santa games and buffet meals. But I could tell yours was a classy group as soon as I saw that woman's black pearl earrings."

"You mean Sharon's?"

"Yes, Sharon's. And I could tell from the vibe in the room, you know, from just how much fun everyone seemed to be having, that you must treat your staff well." She appeared pleased by this observation.

"Here's my resumé, Ms. . . . ?"

"Wilson," she said.

"Here's my resumé, Ms. Wilson." I offered her a crisp sheet of ivory paper. "I understand you're looking for a communications manager. My contact information is all there." She took my resumé and folded it. "Thank you for a truly unexpected evening," I said, already doubting whether I wanted to work for a multinational cell phone company. I'd been attracted to the intimacy of the gathering and convinced myself that its stylish guests worked for a boutique operation. It turned out to be a private party for the top sales representatives in the city; the company itself had thousands of employees.

I offered my hand to Ms. Wilson.

"For real?" she said, reaching instead for the restaurant door.

"My schedule's quite flexible," I blurted, not wanting to waste this precious face-to-face moment with a potential employer. "I could come in for an interview. Just about any time works for me."

"Right," she snorted. "I'll have my receptionist set one up."

I'd hoped Hatim — who turned out to be not Italian but Algerian — would pursue me, maybe leave unnoticed through the kitchen and escort me home. I walked slowly, to give him time to catch up. He had shaggy hockey hair and a twice-broken nose, which, in combination with a pair of weighty cufflinks, had poisoned my common sense. I hadn't planned to get so carried away. Aligning myself with the office flirt had been tactical, the quickest means to learn the ranks in the room and attain the crucial introductions. It had worked in the past. But Hatim possessed an in-your-face charm. His advances were disarmingly straightforward, not at all what I'd prepared for. There was no time or need, it seemed, for flirty sparring. He'd placed one hand on the small of my back, smoothed the static from my hair, and whispered such a stern barrage of compliments that I forgot my purpose in that tinsel-bedecked room.

When it became clear that Hatim had been held up at the restaurant, I began to walk normally, at the pace determined by the mathematics of my body and the height of my heels. The sidewalk was nicked with frost. With each inhalation tiny barbs of ice pricked my lungs, a sensation that was not unpleasant. It felt extraordinary to be out walking so late at night. A guy on a unicycle was the only other person about. He pedalled expertly in my direction and proceeded to ride jerky circles around me while I walked.

"Good to see you're wearing a helmet," I said.

"Always," he said. "You never know when you might encounter a bump in the road." He rode away from me, hopped on and off the curb a couple of times, and then resumed circling me.

"Impressive," I said.

"That's nothing."

The first of the three buses I would need to take to get home surged past en route to its stop outside the twenty-four-hour Souvlaki Shack a few blocks away. I considered running for it, but a window display of handbags sprouting colourful wings distracted me.

"Look at that," I said, walking up to the glass. "What does it even mean?"

"A purse is a pretty bird to wear on your arm?" the unicyclist offered.

While I was stationary, he maintained his balance by scooting his wheel a little bit forward and a little bit back, the way cyclists do at stoplights to prevent their feet touching the ground. A few insignificant snowflakes began to fall. I turned from the display and began walking again, wondering if there would be any phone messages from prospective employers waiting for me at home. I had delivered so many resumés over the past couple of weeks that I couldn't even remember all of the jobs I was hoping to land. I had applied for everything from probation officer to pastry chef, director of marketing for a prestigious chain of hotels to hip-hop dance instructor, and no one had called me back. In my cover letters I indicated my willingness to enrol in any necessary training. I wasn't sure what else I could be doing, where I was going wrong.

The guy on the unicycle lagged behind a ways and then caught up with me. "I was hoping I wouldn't have to ask," he said, "but don't you recognize me?" He popped off his sculpted seat and stood before me, as if stillness might aid my memory. He was slightly taller than me and fully outfitted in thermal wear. He was dressed much more appropriately than I in my snug cocktail dress and symbolic coat.

"I'm sorry," I said.

He looked disappointed.

"A hint?" I said.

"Let me think."

"Can you think and ride? My ankles are numb."

I recalled the contents of my knapsack — jeans, sneakers, scarf, and coat — which I'd left in a corner of Randy's office earlier that afternoon and wouldn't be able to retrieve until the New Year. What had I been thinking? I would need those things. I needed them now.

Randy was the hyper-exercised employment counsellor I'd been seeing weekly for the past two months. I, or should I say my "case," had been assigned to him by a government agency whose aim it was to help people find work, meaningful or otherwise. I'd been let go from my last job as an optometrist's receptionist when it was discovered I'd stopped answering the phone. I'd grown fearful of people, of not knowing the answers to the questions they asked. I switched off the ringer and responded to phone messages and email inquires only, thus affording myself the time to compose thorough replies.

Either Randy wasn't very good at his job or I was completely unemployable. We were getting frustrated with each other. At our appointment earlier that day he'd sighed openly as I detailed the jobs I'd applied for that week, something he never used to do.

"What's wrong?" I snapped partway through my list.

"Nothing, nothing at all," he said. "Please continue. This is great."

I'd also managed to provoke in him a disturbing habit. As he explained why he thought my attempts at finding work were in fact the opposite — self-sabotage was his exact word — he tugged at his eyebrows.

"Do you honestly think you'll fare better in these positions?" Randy asked, hands upturned in question, a few short dark hairs still attached to one of his fingers.

His office was part of a larger suite and the corner where we met was defined by partitions. It was the kind of space that could be cleared out overnight. I wondered if he ever questioned his own job security.

"You need to quit wasting your energy applying for these ridiculous jobs," he said. "We need to determine where you'll be comfortable, where you'll thrive."

Even though we'd obviously done away with pretense, I was still too scared to ask where he thought this thriving might occur: a stockroom in an electronics warehouse where human interaction was minimal, a department store cafeteria with its linear layout and repetitive tasks? And, honestly, I didn't think the jobs I was applying for were ridiculous. I could truly visualize myself in any one of those roles — life coach, radio DJ, marine biologist — and I believed that the talent it took to perform them might switch on inside me, given the chance.

"That, right there," Randy said, "is the problem with your generation. You believe in switches and chances."

The electric cables above the street started to buzz, signalling the approach of another bus. I walked faster. "Listen," I said to the unicyclist riding quietly at my side, "I need to catch this bus."

"Oh, no," he said, "you can't."

"Can and will."

"But things are about to change." He fluttered his hands metamorphically. "Romantically, I mean, things are about to get very romantic."

"I've already had some of that tonight. Maybe you're thinking of someone else."

"That wasn't romance," he sneered. "That was drunken groping."

"You were spying on me?"

"You weren't being very discreet."

I wondered what Hatim's co-workers thought of me, if they would welcome me into the fold or if I'd already sunk my reputation. It occurred to me that Ms. Wilson might have seen us at our sloppiest, passing olives back and forth with our tongues.

"The future," the unicyclist said.

"What?"

"That's your hint."

An empty bus revved past without slowing at its designated stop. I walked and he cycled a while in silence. The bare boulevard trees were strung with white lights. They looked tragic, like adorned anorexics. It was snowing steadily now and because there was no wind the flakes drifted perfectly downward, each puff of molecules agreeing absolutely with gravity. I found this reassuring. Also the click of my heels on concrete was undeniable.

"The future," I repeated.

"Yep," the unicyclist said smugly.

"Can you see the future?"

"Only one aspect of it."

"Does this aspect concern me?"

He touched his nose to indicate the affirmative.

"Will I be offered a job this week?"

"Can't say."

"Can't say or don't know?"

"I don't know anything about your future employment. Do you give up?"

"I give up."

"Okay, are you ready for this?"

"Ready," I said.

"I'm your future husband!"

A crowd of bar patrons separated us briefly as they spilled out onto the sidewalk. The unicyclist navigated their loose limbs like a rodeo star. "Yee-haw!" one of the drunkards called.

"You're kidding, right?" I said as the catcalls faded behind us.

"Life partner works too, whichever you prefer."

My nose was running. I tried to wipe it discreetly with the back of my hand.

"Can't you see us together?" he said, his voice betraying a wounded lilt.

"I need a job, not a husband."

We were approaching the Souvlaki Shack. The smell of roasting meat filled the air. It didn't make me hungry though it did make the night feel colder.

"Do you think I ride this unicycle for fun?"

"Don't you?"

"I learned for the occasion. I wanted our story, the one we tell our children about how we met, to be unique."

"It's not really organic then."

"But isn't it romantic?"

A taxi drove slowly past in the newly fallen snow. The passenger unrolled his window, waved and shouted, *Thanks for the memories!* I was fairly certain, from the expensive flash of the cufflink, it was Hatim.

"What if I don't want children?" I said.

"Don't you?"

Following my meeting with Randy earlier that afternoon I'd requested the key to the bathroom and proceeded to change into my tights and cocktail dress. Static clung to the silky fabric and to my hair so I wet my fingers beneath the tap and ran them down my front and back. I pulled three bangles onto my wrist and appreciated the companionable sounds they made as I went about accenting my eyes. I didn't know what I was getting ready for, only that I couldn't face the python's belly that was my basement apartment. For the first week after I moved in, I bought lamps at nearly every second-hand store I passed, lit them with 100-watt bulbs, and still the rooms felt dark, as if the walls themselves were alive, absorbent. But it wasn't just the gloom I was avoiding, I couldn't bear to search the Internet for more job postings only to come up against the phrase *3–5 years experience required*, the clincher in so many listings. Being constantly reminded of how little experience I had in so many fields was demoralizing. I applied a brighter shade of lipstick than was customary for me, smiled dementedly at the mirror, and returned to the office to ask Randy if I could leave my knapsack in the corner until our next session.

"That won't be until the New Year," he said, his leg shaking with a marathoner's impatience. "I'm on holiday as of today, as of like, right now."

"Fine," I said. I wanted to bash him over the head with my purse.

"Put it there."

I nudged my knapsack between a potted plant and a partition.

"Well, happy holidays," he said. "I'd offer you eggnog or something—"

"But it looks like I'm on my way out," I said, finishing his sentence. We were done. I would have to figure out a way to get my bag back without seeing his wind-chapped face again. I doubted he'd make it hard for me.

"Are we having our first fight?" the unicyclist asked. "I'm sorry. We don't have to talk about children yet."

"Listen," I said. "You're sweet—"

"Don't talk to me like we're in a movie."

"Fine. I don't know if you're sweet or not. Will you get off that thing and walk?"

He obliged.

"Your timing's off," I said. "I'm too distracted by my poverty to think about marriage."

"What about the guy at the restaurant?"

"I was using him."

"Well, your timing's off too. Nobody hires before the holidays. You should wait until the New Year. What do you like to do anyway?"

And here was the problem. I believed I was capable of so much but I didn't actually yearn to do anything. There was nothing I'd always dreamed of being, nor had the basic act of living presented me with any thrilling options. I was thirty, half-naked on the first day of winter. My legs were anaesthetized stumps. I watched my feet fall one in front of the other as if I had nothing to do with them. We'd passed the Souvlaki Shack and had almost reached the Granville Street bridge.

"Shall we cross?" the unicyclist asked.

"I don't have a choice." I hadn't seen a bus pass in some time; they must have quit running for the night.

"What would make this better?" he said. "Or at least tolerable."

"If you told me your car was parked nearby."

"Next best thing."

"If you gave me your gloves."

He quickly offered them. The fleece was warm and dry as an animal's burrow. I wanted to crawl inside, sleep all winter, and wake at that heartening point in nature programs with the first signs of spring: buds unfurling in time-lapse photography, snowmelt, shaky-legged deer.

Crossing the bridge we walked not side by side but single file, him in front so that it seemed like I was following, that we were companions of some kind headed to a common destination. I thought this manoeuvre quite sly but said nothing. When we reached the middle I looked down to where a tide pressed darkly through the channel like blood through a vein. The unicyclist pointed out a community of houseboats. I thought about running away from him. I thought about grabbing his shoulders and ramming my tongue down his throat. I didn't know which impulse was real. Smoke waved like a lover's handkerchief from the chimney of one of the houseboats. I said, "I bet it's cozy in there."

On the other side of the bridge I calculated I was approximately one-third of the way home and probably wouldn't die. We began the trudge up Granville Street, a thoroughfare normally so bloated with traffic that it was eerie to see it abandoned, transformed by the snow into a pointless white chute. The unicyclist held his bike by the seat post and steered it at his side. I watched him out of the corner of my eye.

"What if I told you there was something interesting going on?" he said. "Would you consider a detour?"

First of all, how did he know what constituted a detour for me? Secondly, how could there possibly be something interesting going on, we appeared to be the only two people left on earth.

"Think of it as a stopover," he said. "Besides, you need to warm up."

"Has this been your plan all along?"

"No, and it's probably a bad idea, the last place I should take you. A friend of mine is the organizer. More than one woman has described him as the most handsome man in the city. It's actually very stupid of me to take you there."

"All right," I said. "Let's go." I liked that he was willing to risk losing my attention in order to show me this place, it demonstrated generosity, and the exertion of walking uphill had kindled faint quiverings of heat inside me, making a detour seem possible.

"What if you fall in love?" he said.

"With your friend? Then you should be happy for us."

"I doubt that very much."

We turned down 8th Avenue, past the hulking Masonic Temple, then along blocks of rotting townhomes cloaked in blue tarps. I counted parking metres as we walked and thought about the commissionaire who patrolled my street with a handheld electronic device that spat out violation tickets. It wouldn't make me any friends, but I could do that job, maybe they needed people. Gradually the townhomes gave way to squat office buildings leased by chiropractors and laser surgeons, and shortly after that we found ourselves in an industrial area, block after block of windowless concrete buildings with loading bays.

The unicyclist stopped outside a warehouse. Aside from the disturbed snow — a grey mash of footprints before the doors — I saw nothing to indicate that anything notable, spearheaded by the most handsome man in the city no less, was under way inside.

"What is it?" I said.

"A solstice celebration."

"It's quiet. Maybe it's over now." Just then a door opened and a group of duffle-coated figures shuffled out. In the same moment a couple, heads bowed, came silently from behind us and slipped through the closing door.

"Well?" he said.

"At least I know you haven't lured me here to kill me."

His jaw dropped.

"Kidding," I said. "But look around, you have to admit."

He ignored me and began making his way inside.

It wasn't a warehouse but a gymnasium with waxy floors and basketball hoops at either end of the room. The lights were off and at first glance the floor appeared to be scattered with lanterns, but when I looked more closely I saw there was a pattern, some organizing principle, and that they weren't lanterns, exactly, but brown paper lunch bags with candles inside.

"A labyrinth," the unicyclist whispered. The room was silent except for a droning noise, the sound of someone running a wand around the rim of a huge water-filled bowl. We took our place last in line, behind a dozen people waiting to enter the labyrinth.

"I set it up earlier today," he whispered. "Beeswax, the candles are all made of beeswax. Seven hundred of them."

A woman at the start of the labyrinth was controlling the line, waving people in with a droopy cedar bough. I wasn't sure I would make it. Any warmth my body had conjured on the walk here had vanished and once again cold feathered through me like a hairy underwater weed.

The unicyclist removed his helmet, clipped the chinstraps to his belt and ran his hands through his hair. He sighed and shifted his weight. Finally he touched my elbow and said,

"At least tell me you remember an interview with the Solstice Society."

I didn't.

"My interview was right after yours. Don't you remember sitting together on that papier-mâché couch?"

I did remember a long wait on a wickedly hard couch. "That was papier-mâché?"

"You left a copy of your resumé, which is how I know things about you, like where you live."

"You got the job?" I said, my voice leaping above the hush.

"Yes," he mouthed apologetically.

I took a step back and looked at him intently. He wasn't bad-looking. He had a broad face and earnest, asymmetrical eyes. But no, I didn't remember him.

The line jolted forward and we arrived at the front. No one was behind us; we were the last two people of the night. The gatekeeper ushered us though with a tired sweep of her branch. Inside the labyrinth I found myself, once again, following him, only this time I didn't care. He demonstrated how to walk — arms at your sides, palms open to the floor, a gesture I took to be symbolic of letting go, discarding all your junk from the previous year. I quickly discovered it was also the best way to absorb the warmth, the incredible heat funnelling out of those paper bags. The stiffness melted from my arms and my legs bowed beneath me like saplings. In among the perambulating crowd of parkas and rubber boots I felt embarrassed in my swishy dress and kitten heels, but of course no one was looking at me. Everyone was walking this contrived path for himself. I tried to do the same — surely I had some purging to do — but instead I wondered about the kind of guy who spent his afternoon making lanterns and then rode a unicycle through downtown in search of someone he'd met only once, someone who didn't recognize him at all and gave him very little encouragement in return.

"I don't know why they hired you instead of me," I said over his shoulder. "I could have done this job."

"Of course you could have. My friend put in a good word. It really is who you know. Stop worrying so much, something will happen."

They were words that would have sounded dismissive coming from anyone else but that struck me as hopeful coming from him. Maybe I was drunk on the heat and the pagan glow, or just incredibly tired. If he was more goofy than romantic he was nonetheless dear and determined and I could appreciate that in a man, in anyone. I looked around for his notoriously handsome friend.

"Where is he?" I said.

"I'd be an idiot to point him out."

But the truth was everyone looked beautiful in that light, in all their excruciating concentration. I knew I should be looking inward, but I was too curious about what everyone else was emptying from their open hands. I wanted to gather up all their grievances and humiliations and regrets and examine them. I wanted to measure them against my own.

When we reached the centre of the labyrinth we stood together and closed our eyes. I hadn't purged anything. I didn't feel renewed. But the room smelled sweet, beeswax sweet, terrifically so.

Acknowledgements

THANK YOU to the warm and wonderful Samantha Haywood for believing in these stories and finding an ideal home for them with Freehand Books. Thank you to the passionate team at Freehand—Deborah Willis for her favourable reception, Barbara Scott for her astute editorial guidance, Kelsey Attard for her keen copyeditor's eye, and Anna Boyar for her enthusiasm and thoughtfulness at every turn. Also to Natalie Olsen of Kisscut Design for the stunning cover and book design.

Thank you to Lorna Jackson, your fiction workshop was a revelation. Thank you to my friends and teachers at UBC for the community and encouragement.

The stories in this collection have, at various stages, landed in the laps of the following people, those who've offered their friendship and feedback over the years: Megan Adam, Théodora Armstrong, Catharine Chen, Doretta Lau, Anne-Mary Mullen, Jill Margo, Nancy Mauro, Susan Mersereau, Emily Milliken, Nadine Pederson, Zoey Leigh Peterson, and Ivy Young. Thank you also to Hal Wake for urging me to collect my stories in book form. The entire Vancouver Writers Fest team has been ceaselessly supportive.

Earlier versions of these stories were published in magazines: "Chaperone" in *Grain* and *The Journey Prize Stories 20*; "Split" in *The Malahat Review* and *The Journey Prize Stories 18*; "Juvenile" in *The Fiddlehead*, *The Journey Prize Stories 26*, and *Coming Attractions 13*; "What Are You Good At, What

Do You Like to Do?" in *Prairie Fire* and *Coming Attractions 13*; "Lamb" in *Coming Attractions 13*. Thank you to the editors of these magazines for the opportunity to appear in your fine pages, and to Mark Anthony Jarman for selecting my work for *Coming Attractions 13*.

I'm grateful to the Canada Council for the Arts for financial assistance.

There is no adequate expression of gratitude I can offer my parents, Patricia and Terence, my first and best readers and general cheerleaders in life. Your love has made everything possible.

Thank you to the Campbell/Ross clan in Victoria for the ongoing hilarity and the odd detail, and to my brother, Liam, for his quiet confidence in my endeavors.

And finally, thank you to Jude for waking me up to life and for surprising me every day, and to Cole, whose belief in me has always been unwavering and whom I've loved for more years than I have not.

Notes

The Lantern Society in "What Are You Good At, What Do You Like to Do?" is inspired by Vancouver's Secret Lantern Society: www.secretlantern.org.

The birthing model in "Congratulations & Regrets" was inspired by one used for medical training at the BC Women's Hospital & Health Centre.

CLEA YOUNG's stories have been included in *The Journey Prize Stories* three times. Her work has appeared in *Event, Grain, The Fiddlehead, The Malahat Review, Prairie Fire,* and *Room.* She lives with her husband and son in Vancouver, British Columbia.